Susan Carlisle's love affair with books began in the sixth grade, when she made a bad grade in mathematics. Not allowed to watch TV until she'd brought the grade up, Susan filled her time with books. She turned her love of reading into a passion for writing, and now has over ten Medical Romances published through Mills & Boon. She writes about hot, sexy docs and the strong women who captivate them. Visit SusanCarlisle.com.

THE BROODING SURGEON'S BABY BOMBSHELL

SUSAN CARLISLE

MILLS & BOON

Published in Great Britain 2018
by Mills & Boon, an imprint of HarperCollins*Publishers*
1 London Bridge Street, London, SE1 9GF

© 2018 Susan Carlisle AW

ISBN: 978-0-263-07645-5

MIX
Paper from
responsible sources
FSC C007454

This book is produced from independently certified FSC™ paper
to ensure responsible forest management.
For more information visit www.harpercollins.co.uk/green.

Printed and bound in Great Britain
by CPI Group (UK) Ltd, Croydon, CR0 4YY

To Jeanie.

The best sister-in-law I could have ever wished for.

PROLOGUE

THEIR NIGHT OF passion had started so innocently.

Dr. Gabriel Marks had taken the only open seat at the dining table. The petite young woman with the light brown hair and quick wit he remembered from the committee meeting six months earlier sat to one side of him. She smiled and said hello, as did the rest of the committee members.

Their chairperson had organized the dinner for those members flying in that evening. The next day they would all be attending the meeting at the High Hotel at Chicago's O'Hare Airport.

As a transplant surgeon, Gabe was honored to serve on the liver committee of the National Organ Allocation Network. The group met twice yearly to discuss issues involving liver donation and policy. The professionals who made up the committee, as well as family members of patients, came from all over the country and represented different areas of liver transplantation. What they did was important and saved lives.

If he remembered correctly, the woman dining beside him was Zoe somebody, a former registered nurse who now worked for the Liver Alliance, a group that educated people with liver disease and assisted patients needing a liver transplant. The Liver Alliance did good work. He'd had some dealings with the group in the past regarding patients with special considerations, but he'd never met Zoe before joining the committee.

The discussion around the table was lively during their meal and he appreciated Zoe's quick wit and infectious laugh.

The next morning, they had acknowledged each with a warm hello but had sat on opposite sides of the table during the six-hour meeting. When Zoe had spoken up, her remarks had been intelligent, enlightened and spot-on. He'd been impressed.

After the meeting had adjourned he'd headed to the airport to catch his plane home. But his quick check of the flight board revealed his plane had been grounded because of thunderstorms. Gabe was watching the word *Canceled* cascade down the panel when a groan of dismay had him turning around. It was Zoe.

She looked at him, her face screwed up. "Sorry. I hadn't meant to be so loud. This wasn't in my plans."

"It never is," Gabe responded.

"You're right about that." She looked up and down the concourse. "I guess I'm going to spend the night in the airport."

"I bet if we hurry we can get a room in the hotel before everyone figures out what's going on." Gabe turned back the way they had come.

"A room?" Her voice squeaked.

He gave her a pointed look. "I meant a room apiece. Are you always so literal?"

She grinned, walking past him at a fast clip. "I knew what you meant. I just wanted a head start if there was only one left."

He chuckled and hurried to catch up with her. A short time later they had rooms for the night. As they walked toward the elevator Gabe said, "I'm sorry, but I've racked my brain and still can't come up with your last name."

"Avery. Zoe Avery." She chuckled. "That came out sounding a little James Bondish, didn't it?"

He laughed. "Maybe a little bit. Would you like to meet for supper? Unless you have other plans." He rarely had a night free of paperwork and he wasn't going to spend this one by himself. Not when he liked this woman and was fairly confident she'd accept his invitation.

They entered the elevator. "What other plans would I have but to channel surf?" she answered with a grin.

Her mischievous talk appealed to him. As a transplant surgeon at a San Francisco hospital, he didn't have many people in his life who dared to speak to him so freely. He found it refreshing.

The elevator doors opened. As she prepared to exit, he held the doors open. "Meet you at seven in the hotel restaurant?"

"There's not a wife who's going to be mad at me, is there?" Her playful grin belied the serious concern in her eyes. Had a date ever lied to her about being married?

"No wife. How about your husband?"

"No. Not one of those either." There was a sad note in her reply, yet she cheerfully confirmed, "See you at seven, then." She waved as he stepped out.

Gabe took a moment to appreciate the gentle feminine sway of her hips, anticipating the evening to come.

He was waiting at the restaurant entrance when Zoe strolled up. There was a bright smile on her face. "Sorry, I didn't have anything else to wear." She brushed a hand across the front of the simple navy dress she'd been wearing earlier in the day.

"You look great to me." And she did. Something about her pulled at him. He wanted to know her better.

She grinned. "Thanks. You know the right thing to say to a stranded woman."

He chuckled. "If we have to be stuck somewhere, I'm glad it's a place with hot running water."

"I'm surprised you didn't say food."

"Now that you mention it, that's important too. Our table won't be ready for a few minutes. Would you like to wait in the bar?"

"Sure." Zoe walked ahead of him. She was a tiny thing with a powerful personality.

He ordered their drinks and carried them to a small table. They sat and talked about that day's meeting until the waiter came to get them.

Zoe stood, brushing against him as she moved to avoid someone sitting next to them. Gabe's blood heated. He had no doubt her movements had been unintentional, but his body reacted just the same. It had been some time since a woman had gotten to him on so many levels so quickly.

The waiter showed them to a corner table and handed them menus. They discussed what they would order and were ready when the waiter returned.

After he'd left Gabe remarked, "If I remember correctly, you're a patient advocate with the Liver Alliance and live in the Washington, DC, area."

"That's a good memory. I'm impressed. You were paying attention."

Feeling ashamed, he said, "Apparently not when you said your name."

"It's okay. It happens."

"So have you always been with the Liver Alliance?"

"I went to work in an ICU when I was fresh out of school. I worked a lot with liver patients and really liked it. I decided to go back to school and become a liver transplant coordinator. About a year ago I needed something with regular hours. The Education Chair position came open and it was a perfect fit. Good, stable hours, a tiny office, and I'm still working with the people I love."

Gabe nodded. "And you like living in DC?" He didn't normally quiz his dinner dates, but his curiosity about Zoe was uncharacteristically strong.

"I do. There's always plenty to do. Museums to visit, music festivals and just the excitement of being in the center of our government."

Her enthusiasm for the area was contagious.

She leaned back and looked at him. "And you're from San Francisco. Pretty city."

Obviously, she'd been paying more attention than he had during introductions. "Yep."

"That's a pretty tough commute for these meetings." She ran her finger down the side of her water glass, leaving a trail of condensation.

What would it feel like to have her do that over his chest? He shifted in his chair. They were having dinner. That was all. They didn't really know each other. "I try not to schedule surgery for the day I get back. It makes it easier to deal with the time change." Gabe took a sip of his drink then said, "You seemed pretty upset about not flying out tonight."

"Yeah. My mother has the beginnings of Alzheimer's and I don't like to leave her alone overnight. I'm worried she might not handle being by herself."

"You worked it out?"

"I did. I got a friend to go over and stay with her." Worry flickered in her eyes as she glanced away.

"She's why you needed the job with regular hours. I understand caring for someone with your mother's illness can be difficult." He was an only child whose mother turned to him often for help and emotional support, but she still possessed her mental faculties. If she didn't and he had to provide her with constant care even while he traveled…?

Zoe looked at him again, brow furrowed. "It is. I hate watching her wasting away. And good care is costly."

"My mother is all I've got. My father died before I was born. I can only imagine how I would feel if she got sick."

Her eyes took on a dark look before she said, "Growing up without a father can be tough. Do you have a stepfather?" Zoe seemed to have changed the subject on purpose.

"Nope. Mom never remarried." He'd often wondered why. She'd always said it was because his father had been the love of her life, but he'd thought there might be more to it. As a kid, he had overheard her tell a friend she felt like she might be doing Gabe a disservice by not marrying. That she worried her decision not to do so had left Gabe with no male role model or father figure.

"She must be a great mom," Zoe commented, bringing him back to the present. "You seemed to have turned out all right."

His mother had been and still was a good mother, but truth be known, his grandmother had been the primary adult during his formative years. His mother had worked full-time to provide for him. "Thanks for saying so. But lately she's been applying pressure to become a grandmother. It gets old."

Zoe's head turned to the side, her look quizzical. "You have no interest in making her one?"

"No. I'm not good family material. My job, my career, doesn't leave me any room for a family. I'm far too busy. More than one girlfriend has accused me of being a workaholic. A wife and children deserve a full-time husband and father. I decided long ago that that drama wasn't for me."

A peculiar expression came over her face, but before he could ask what was wrong, the waiter brought their meals. Zoe started talking about places she had visited and would like to go to and he dismissed her unexplainable expression in favor of her entertaining conversation. When they were done with their meal, Gabe said, "It's still early. Would you like to go to the jazz bar downstairs?"

She hesitated a moment. It really mattered to Gabe that she said yes. She finally quipped, "Why not? It sounds like fun."

Relief washed over him and he smiled. Why was it so important that she go? He placed his hand at her back and guided her out of the restaurant toward the circular stairs. His hand fit perfectly in the hollow of her back. At the club, he asked for a table close to the band.

They had been there a few minutes when Zoe touched his arm. She leaned in close and said into his ear, "I needed this. Thanks for asking me."

He smiled, glad she was having a good time. His body tightened with awareness. It was overreacting, big-time. Or was *he* overly conscious of his body's natural response to an attractive woman he genuinely liked? They were both single and old enough to know their own minds, so why shouldn't they enjoy each other's attention?

Several couples moved to the open area of the floor. On impulse Gabe asked, "Would you like to dance?"

"I'm not very good." She sounded more disappointed than rejecting.

He stood and offered his hand. "You don't have to be. Just follow my lead."

Zoe smiled. One he would remember. "Hey, I can do that."

Gabe held her hand as they stepped out onto the floor. Pulling her into his arms, his hand went to her waist. It was so small his arm almost wrapped all the way around her. The top of her head came to just below his chin. The sweet scent of her filled his head and his body stirred. He resisted the strong urge to pull her tight, but firmly squelched the idea. His arousal would be evident. This was the nicest evening he'd had in a long time and he had no intention of ruining it by scaring her off.

The sultry sound of the saxophone swirled around them.

She looked up, commanding his attention. "I'm impressed. You've a surgeon's touch even on the dance floor, gentle and skilled."

"Thank you, ma'am." He brought her a little closer in spite of his resolve. There were other things he was good at he'd like to show her. He needed to squelch those types of thoughts too. Gabe missed a step.

Her hand squeezed his shoulder when she stumbled.

He looked at her, mumbling, "Sorry."

"I'm sure it's your partner," she said.

Searching the depths of her eyes, he muttered, "I assure you it isn't."

"I've not had much opportunity to dance since my prom, years ago."

Her eyes were so green. "You're doing great."

She stared back. They continued to move slowly around the space. It wasn't until there was a mumble going around the room that he forced his attention away from her seductive gaze. The music had stopped. They were the only ones still on the dance floor.

Zoe looked around. Her cheeks were spots of red. "Oops. I guess we got carried away." She focused on him. "It's been a long day and time I head upstairs. It's later in my time zone than it is in yours."

"Okay." Gabe hated to let her go. He held her hand as they returned to the table. She picked up her bag and he left a few bills on the table for their drinks. "I'll see you to your room."

Zoe grasped her bag with both hands. He would have liked to have one of them in his. Somehow it seemed to belong there. What would she do if he kissed her? Would she push him away? Did he dare take a chance? He'd regret it if he didn't.

They entered the elevator and rode up to her floor without a word. The need to touch her, hold her gnawed at him. Tension, thick as a wool blanket in the winter, lay between them. She glanced at him once, her soft, questioning eyes uncertain. He was painfully aware of what he wanted but did she feel the same? The decision must be hers.

At her door, she pulled her keycard from her purse and turned to face him. "Thank you. I really enjoyed this evening. Especially the dancing."

Was she flirting with him? Testing the water?

She gave him a long look as if reaching a decision. With a blink, her hands came to rest on his shoulders as she stood on her toes and kissed him.

That was all the encouragement Gabe needed. He reached out, pulling her against him, his mouth crushing hers, his tongue finding a warm welcome. Her arms wrapped his neck and she hung on during the most passionate kiss he'd ever received. He wanted her. Right now. Based on her actions, she wouldn't deny him.

He steadied her on her feet and growled, "Key."

Zoe put it in his hand, her lips finding his again. He had no problem with that. Backing her against the door and with a minimum amount of fumbling, he managed to get the door opened and them inside.

It closed with a click behind them. Zoe's legs wrapped around his waist. His hands cupped her butt as he stumbled toward the bed, his blood boiling and his body alive with desire for her.

He eased her down onto the mattress, moving over her. Had he ever been this hot for a woman? Supporting himself on his hands, he searched her face. She stared back.

He saw the second doubt creep in. Gabe gently kissed her. "I want you. Badly."

Silent for a moment, she whispered, "Make me feel good tonight, Gabe. Forget everything."

"I can do that." His mouth took hers while his hands worked to remove her clothes.

She followed suit with equal frenzy. Her moans of desire combined with the kneading of her fingers on his bare back made him more aroused than he'd ever believed possible. Their mating was blistering, fast and very, very satisfying.

Hours later Gabe rolled over. His hand brushed warm, soft skin. *Zoe.* His body stirred once more. He wanted her again.

"Mmm…" she murmured before her kisses teased his chest.

His hand skimmed the rise of her hip. "Damn, I don't have another condom."

Her hand brushed his length as she murmured, "I'm on the pill."

Unable to go without her any longer, he saw to her pleasure then found his. Having no barrier between them felt so right.

When he woke again, Zoe was dressed and stuffing her belongings into her luggage. "Where're you going?"

"I have to catch my plane." Her back remained to him.

"You've already rescheduled?" He was still in a haze.

"They texted me." She did glance at him then. "I have to go. I need to get home to Mom."

Gabe could see the glass wall rising between them. Unbreakable. All the warmth they had shared last night was now frigid air. Zoe was embarrassed by her behavior. It shouldn't bother him. He wasn't looking for forever, but he didn't like the idea of being something she regretted.

"Zoe—"

"I have to go." She was out the door before he could untangle the sheets from his body.

CHAPTER ONE

ZOE CLUTCHED THE restroom door handle in the conference area of the High Hotel. It had been almost six months since she'd seen Gabe and she was hiding from him. She suspected he was impatiently waiting for her in the hall. Not facing him wasn't a choice she had. Her entire world had changed in that amount of time. Her mother was worse. And Zoe was pregnant.

Guilt hung on her like a heavy necklace of stones she wore all the time. She should have told Gabe. It wouldn't have been that hard to contact him. She'd used him to escape her life for a night and now there was a baby to consider. He'd deserved better on a number of levels. When she'd kissed him at her hotel-room door she hadn't planned on becoming the "drama" he had been adamant about not having in his life.

He knew now. He'd seen her protruding belly when she'd stood. She'd heard his gasp from halfway across the meeting room. There had been no mistaking his shocked expression when she'd glanced back. Would he care if it was his? Did he want to know? Regardless, he deserved to be told he was going to be a father. Even though he'd stated a family wasn't for him.

She paused before pulling the door open. Hopefully Gabe had already returned to the committee room. At first she had thought the stomach rolling had been a virus.

After a few weeks she'd had to admit it might be something else. But couldn't believe it. She'd been taking the pill. She'd dragged her feet about buying a pregnancy test because she'd just been unable to wrap her mind around the idea she might be expecting. She'd thought of contacting Gabe the moment she'd seen the test was positive, but had immediately found an excuse not to. Each time she'd convinced herself she had to tell him, she'd come up with a reason not to call him. Too tired, working too late, her mother needed her right that minute, and the list went on. The truth was Gabe had said he wasn't interested in being a father and she felt guilty for her part in involving him.

How would he react when he found out? She'd vowed after each of their committee's monthly conference calls to call and tell him. As time had gone by, she'd decided he deserved to hear the news face-to-face. Their semiannual in-person meeting was soon and she'd planned to tell him then. What she hadn't counted on was not seeing him the night before. She'd fully expected to have a chance to tell him in private before their committee meeting. Sadly that hadn't happened.

Her fingers flexed on the handle. What if Gabe had found someone special since they had been together? The idea disturbed her more than it should have. Any relationship he might have could be hurt when the woman learned of the baby. Just another reason Zoe shouldn't have put off telling him. She hadn't intended to hurt him. Ever.

Was he mad? Glad? Would he believe it was his? She'd been such a coward.

Her body had hummed with tension all morning as she'd anticipated telling Gabe. More than once she'd had to remind herself to breathe. Had even had to force herself to eat a bite or two of the croissant she'd gotten off the breakfast buffet. Despite being five months along, morning food still didn't always agree with her. Her temperamental tummy was made worse by nerves strung so taut they would hit a high note if plucked.

She had glanced at Gabe several times. His gaze had met hers on a number of those. When it had, ripples of pleasurable awareness had zinged through her. She wasn't sure if it was the flapping of wings in her belly or the baby kicking, but her body had a definite reaction to the sight of him. She was still attracted to him. There had been an uneasiness in his eyes, but a glint of pleasure as well. Had he been glad to see her before she'd stood up, revealing her condition?

Their night together had been memorable. Extremely delightful and erotic. She'd let go like she'd never allowed herself to do before. Her life had been becoming more complicated and she'd just wanted to live a little. Gabe was there, tall, dark and handsome with a Southern drawl, her fantasy come to life…almost.

Her dream man would want to marry and have a family.

Yet despite that one character flaw, she'd wanted Gabe to give her the attention she'd craved. Had been greedy about it. Being with him had made her feel alive, desirable and carefree. She'd taken shameless advantage of their night of passion. The fear it might not come her way again had had her agreeing to things she was normally cautious about.

Not only was Gabe easy on the eyes but intelligent, thoughtful, funny and a great conversationalist. He really listened. She liked him, too much. Now fate had them in its grasp. Like it or not, against all odds, they were having a child together.

Finding the right man had been difficult for her. She refused to settle or compromise. She wanted a man devoted to her, who would feel the same way about their family. More than once her mother had said Zoe was dreaming of someone who didn't exist. Zoe resisted that idea, knowing her mother was jaded from being an abandoned wife and mother. Still, Zoe believed there could be a happily ever after out there for her. She just had to find the right man.

The one time Zoe had thought she had, she'd ended up devastated. While confident their relationship had been progressing toward marriage, she'd caught Shawn having dinner with another woman. When she'd confronted him, he'd announced they didn't want the same things out of life. That no man could live up to her expectations. That Zoe had an unrealistic view of life and relationships. To believe a man could be devoted to just one woman was antiquated.

Other men had implied the same thing. She still vowed not to lower her standards, even when she realized her pledge might mean she'd never have the family she'd dreamed of. Gabe's assertion about not being interested in a wife or family only meant he wasn't any different than the other men she'd been interested in. They'd all been like her father and left when life had turned inconvenient.

She'd fully accepted Gabe was not Mr. Right when she'd let go of her inhibitions that night, confident in her birth control.

Zoe lightly banged her forehead against the bathroom door, her hand aching from the prolonged tight grip on the handle. She just wanted that one man who would love her forever. If that was being too picky, so be it. As her mother's condition gradually deteriorated, it was becoming more difficult to date, even if she had a chance. At least now, with a baby on the way, she had one of the two things she'd always wanted.

With a sudden surge of resolution, Zoe gripped the handle even tighter, her knuckles going white. She had to face Gabe. It was time. She ran her free hand over the rise at her middle, unable to keep the smile from forming despite her anxiety. When she had finally accepted she was pregnant, she'd been filled with joy. The only disappointment was that she didn't have a husband to share her happiness with.

She rolled her shoulders back, forcing them to relax, took a fortifying breath and stepped out into the hallway. As she suspected, Gabe was there. Waiting.

Gabe gasped when Zoe stood. He felt like he'd just been sucker punched in the gut. His throat constricted as his heart recovered and went into high gear, pounding like a drum against his ribs.

Zoe was *pregnant!*

It was obvious beneath her pink dress.

For the past two hours she'd been sitting across from him, so involved in their committee's discussion she hadn't left the table. At least he'd assumed that was why she hadn't stood until the midmorning break.

Gabe clamped his mouth shut and swallowed, trying to slow his thundering heart. Tearing his gaze from Zoe's rounded middle, he glanced wildly about the conference room. *Was it his?*

Numerous times over the last months he'd thought of her. Of their night together. More than once he'd picked up his phone with the intention of calling her, only to put it down, afraid his intrusion into her life wouldn't be welcomed, especially after the way she had left the morning after.

He'd hoped to get to the hotel earlier so he could talk to her but his flight hadn't cooperated. His surgery schedule hadn't either. Instead of coming in the night before, he'd had to take a morning plane.

After he'd gasped, Zoe had glanced back at him before she'd hurried toward the conference-room exit. *Was she running from him again?*

Standing, he'd pushed his chair away with so much

force he'd had to catch it before he could make his way around the table. He'd been stopped by one of the other committee members but had ended that conversation in short order.

He'd stalked down the hall toward the restrooms, his best guess for where she'd gone.

It could be someone else's.

His heart did another tap dance. Zoe could have found someone just after they'd been together. He shook his head. His gut told him that wasn't the case. Maybe it was the way he'd caught her uncertain look before she'd headed from the room.

The unending fascination he still felt for her hadn't been part of his plan for a one-night stand, but it was there anyway. Now it appeared that night had had bigger repercussions than the memories that haunted him.

Gabe stationed himself across from the women's restroom. Zoe had to come out sometime.

When the door finally opened, Zoe stepped into the hall and Gabe met her in the middle of it. Despite the large area around them, the space seemed to zoom inward until it was just he and Zoe.

"Is it mine?" His words were low and harsh.

She nodded, before she looked away then back to him. "You don't have to worry. I can take care of it. I won't make any demands on you."

Gabe's head jerked back in disbelief. "What? Of course I'll help. This is my child too."

"It was an accident. I can take care of us." Her hand brushed her middle. "You don't need to feel obligated in any way. I just wanted you to know about the baby." Her voice grew stronger and she tried to step around him.

He blocked her path. "Yes, I can tell how eager you were to tell me. Must have been damned near impossible for you to keep it a secret all these months." He almost winced at the sarcasm in his voice. "You should have told me. Not blindsided me."

Zoe put a protective hand on her middle. Her eyes turned sad. "I wanted to. Tried. Sorry."

At the sound of footsteps, they both glanced up the hall in the direction of the committee room. It was one of the other members coming their direction.

"Please, let's not make a scene," Zoe begged.

Gabe took her elbow. He was gentle yet firm. "Come. We need to talk." He led her to a small alcove some distance down the hall from the restrooms.

Bile rose in his throat as Zoe stepped as far away from him as the space would allow. Just months ago, she'd been so alive in his arms. He took a deep breath in an effort to regain control, perspective.

"This isn't the time or the place for this." The desperation in her eyes and tone was unmistakable.

He glared at her. "Would you have ever told me if you hadn't had to? Did you really think I wouldn't notice? Did you manage to forget I've seen all of you, knew your body down to the smallest detail?"

Heat filled her cheeks. It was plain she remembered as well as he did, perhaps more clearly.

Gabe watched her closely. "Why didn't you tell me?"

Her hand went over her middle again. "This wasn't supposed to happen. I take full responsibility. I just thought you deserved to be told to your face."

"It seems to me that you could have at least picked up the phone and called."

"I know I should have, but I just kept making excuses. Then I knew I was going to see you here, but you didn't come to the dinner last night…"

The tension in his shoulders eased. She must be under a lot of pressure. Could he believe her? "I got stuck in surgery. Look, you're right. Now isn't the time for us to talk. We're expected back in the meeting. When does your plane leave?"

"Just after the meeting." Zoe glanced at the opening as if anxious to leave.

His voice softened. "You can't change it?"

"No. I have to get home to see about my mother. Just being gone overnight has become a problem. I've got to go." She shifted toward the opening.

"Okay. We'll have to figure something out later. But we *will* talk." He nodded his head toward the opening. "Why don't you go back ahead of me? I'll be along in a minute. I'd rather there be as little talk as possible."

With a curt nod of apparent agreement, she slipped past him and hurried away.

He was going to be a father. Gabe's chest had a funny ache in it. Was it joy? Being a father had never been in his plans. He'd always been so careful. Zoe had changed that.

He'd grown up without a father. That had been the deciding factor in his decision to forgo the family route. Yet now that his plans for his life had just been rewritten permanently, he was determined no child of his would grow up not knowing his father. Zoe could protest that he wasn't obligated all she liked. If she'd thought that feeble opposition would make him walk off as if nothing had ever happened, she'd badly underestimated him.

More annoying still was his body's reaction to her nearness. She'd been standing so close. Her soft floral scent still lingered in his nostrils. That fragrance would forever be hers. Memories washed over him. Zoe soft and willing in his arms. The sweet, lilting moan she'd made as they'd joined. It was a night he'd replayed over and over in his mind. Yet this wasn't the outcome he'd planned. But one he would accept. Deal with.

In the last few minutes his world had altered irreversibly. In a few months he would be a father. Next month he would be in a new job. A very visible one. He needed to look professional, be in control of his life. Gabe took a deep breath, gathered his emotions. Life had just grabbed him by the tail.

Zoe made her way back to the conference room on weak knees. Gabe had been right. They didn't need to return at the same time, especially after one of the committee members had caught them arguing. Had the woman over-heard what they'd been talking about? Yet Gabe's sensible suggestion that they enter separately troubled her. Was he ashamed of her?

Maybe it was best. They shouldn't draw attention to themselves, so that they'd have to explain what was going on between them. All she'd planned to do was tell Gabe and now he knew. She didn't expect anything more from him and had made that plain. They would part ways today and that would be it. He'd have his life, his career, on the West Coast and she and the baby theirs on the East.

Except Gabe had said he wanted to talk. Would he be making demands? She had been surprised by the feroc-ity in his tone when he'd stated he would be in his child's life. Where had that come from? Especially after he'd told her he wasn't interested in a family. It must have been the shock of learning he was going to be a father. That was all it was.

She had just settled her shaking body in the chair when the moderator called the meeting back to order. Gabe slipped into his chair a minute later with an apologetic nod in the chairperson's direction. Zoe refused to meet his look, the one she felt on her. The rest of the day would be long. Picking up her pen, she doodled on a page of her agenda to keep herself from glancing at him. The few times she dared to look, his thoughtful light blue gaze was fixed on her. She still found him attractive.

At their lunch break, Gabe started her way but was stopped by someone asking him a question. That gave her the chance to grab her meal and hurry back to her place, avoiding interacting with him again.

By midafternoon the meeting was ending. Zoe hadn't heard much of it. She had been busy berating herself for failing to think through the consequences of not telling Gabe sooner.

"Dr. Marks," the chairperson said, and the room erupted in clapping.

Zoe's head jerked up. What had just been said? She gave a half-hearted pat of her hands as she watched Gabe. He smiled, nodding, as he looked around the room.

His gaze met hers briefly before he said, "Thank you. I look forward to becoming the head of transplants at National Hospital."

The earlier fluttering in her stomach took off like a covey of quail. Gabe would be moving to the East Coast. To the same area as her!

She stared at him in disbelief.

He shrugged.

The rest of the people in the room stood and gathered their belongings. Zoe didn't move. She'd believed Gabe would be three thousand miles away when he'd talked about being involved with their child. Now he would just be down the road. He might want to see the baby not only during the summer, while taking a few weeks of annual vacation, but regularly. He could even want part-time custody. This situation was spinning out of her control.

By the time she pulled her thoughts together, the room was practically empty. Gabe was still being congratulated by a couple of people when she was ready to go. In a stupor of shock, she snatched up her purse and grabbed the suitcase handle, hurrying out, unable to think clearly.

Gabe had upended her envisioned future as a happy single parent.

"Zoe."

She looked over her shoulder to see him striding toward her, and walked faster.

"Wait up," he called.

"I need to catch my plane." She had too much to process. Needed time to think.

Gabe pulled level with her. "But we need to talk."

"If you wanted to talk so badly, why didn't you tell me you had accepted a job that had you moving for all intents and purposes into my backyard?"

His mouth gaped in shock as he grabbed her arm, forcing her to stop.

"Maybe because I was too busy trying to recover from the bomb you dropped on me."

He did have her there. She inhaled and said on the exhalation, "I think we both need some time to consider what we need to do." His touch made her tremble, triggering memories of his hands all over her that night. How was she supposed to think?

"I already know what I want," he snapped. "I intend to be as much a part of my child's life as possible."

"Does it matter what I want?" Zoe jerked free, took hold of her luggage handle again and started out of the hotel attached to the airport by a tunnel that led under the street.

Gabe matched her stride. "You didn't think I'd want to know my child, did you?"

"I thought you deserved to know he or she existed, but I never imagined you'd want to be involved as closely as you're talking about." She kept increasing her pace, lugging her bag behind her. "You made it perfectly clear you weren't family material before we went to bed together."

"Oho, so that's it. You didn't think I'd care about being

a father. It so happens that now that I am one I intend to be one. You have a problem with that?"

"I don't know. I might if you keep applying this much pressure all the time," she hissed.

"If I keep... You've had months to adjust to having a child. I only just learned I'm going to be a father." His frustration was loud and clear.

Guilt assaulted her. "I'm sorry about that. It wasn't fair, but you can't expect me to make a life-changing decision for my child while I'm on the way to the airport."

They continued through the tunnel into the terminal. Gabe remained beside her, larger than life. Why couldn't he give her some space? She was already tied in emotional knots. She needed to get away, get home and regroup.

Zoe had other things to consider besides Gabe's newly found parental outrage. Her friend had just sent a text to say that her mom was anxious, constantly searching the apartment and asking for Zoe.

Her thoughts were too scattered. She needed to consider carefully everything she said or agreed to. What happened would affect her and her child forever. "Gabe, I'm not talking about this right now. You're moving across the country and you need time to get settled into your new job before you agree to shoulder the responsibilities of fatherhood. Responsibilities you need to carefully weigh first. Meanwhile, I need time to handle other issues in my life."

"Is there someone else involved here?" His question was a demand. "Are you involved with someone?"

"No, nothing like that." She glanced at Gabe in time to see him visibly relax. What did it matter to him if she had a boyfriend—or a lover, for that matter?

He touched her elbow to steady her when she rocked back as they headed up the escalators to the security area. Heat zipped through her. "You need to hold the handrail."

"I'm perfectly capable of taking care of myself. Pregnancy doesn't make me feeble-minded." She'd covered her reaction to him with feistiness she didn't completely feel as she pulled her arm from his hand.

"Neither does it mean you shouldn't be careful or unwilling to accept help."

Zoe's look met his. Gabe's didn't waver. He appeared sincerely concerned. She had to admit it was nice to have someone care about her welfare. So much of her life revolved around helping others, her patients and her mother. Being worried over was a pleasant change. They stepped off the escalator and continued down the concourse. "I promise I'll be careful."

She looked ahead. A young woman with a baby strapped to her chest was pushing a rented luggage cart piled high with bags. Standing on the front, holding on, was a boy of about four. Seconds before they passed Zoe, the cart wobbled and the boy fell backward onto the unforgiving floor with a sickening thud. The mother screamed as blood flowed.

Even as the accident registered in Zoe's mind, Gabe was down on one knee beside the child. The boy's screeching echoed off the high glass ceiling as the mother pushed Gabe's shoulder in her effort to reach the boy.

He half turned, catching hold of her as he said in a level, calm manner, "Ma'am, I'm a doctor. Don't move him. You could make it worse. What's his name?"

"Bobby. Bobby's his name," the woman said between crying huffs.

"Bobby, hush. I'm Dr. Gabe. I'm going to help you." Gabe continued to speak softly and reassuringly to the boy.

Zoe noticed a diaper bag sitting on top of the woman's luggage pile. Grabbing it, she opened it and searched until she found a diaper. Laying it as flat as possible on the floor, she carefully slipped it beneath the boy's head, then held his head steady to stop him from squirming.

Gabe nodded to her then said, "Bobby, I need to see if you're hurt anywhere else. Your mom's right here. She can hold your hand, but you must be still."

The boy's crying quieted, although tears continued to roll down his face.

A crowd circled them yet Gabe's full attention remained focused on the child.

The mother moved to the opposite side of the boy, going down on her knees beside Zoe. Taking his small hand, she said, "I'm here, honey." The baby on her chest started to cry and she patted her on the bottom. "Don't cry, Bobby. You're making me and Susie cry too."

The boy gave her a sad smile. His chest shuddered as he struggled to stop sobbing. The mother's eyes were wild with fear as she stared expectantly at Gabe.

"Bobby, do you have a dog?" he asked, reaching for and pulling his suitcase to him.

"Uh-huh." The boy grew quiet and watched Gabe.

Nimbly, Gabe unzipped a side pocket and removed a stethoscope. "What's his name?"

"Marty."

"Marty—that's a good name for a dog. Did you give it to him?"

Zoe shifted closer to the mother. Placing her fingers on the pulse of the boy's wrist, Zoe checked his heart rate.

"One-ten," she told Gabe. Thankfully it wasn't very high.

Zoe looked up to see a security guard hurrying in their direction. When he arrived she said, "I'm a nurse and he's a doctor." She nodded in the direction of Gabe. "Call 911. This boy needs to be seen at a hospital."

Thankfully the man didn't waste time arguing and spoke into his radio.

Meanwhile Bobby was saying, "No, my mom did. I wanted to name him Purple."

Gabe grinned. "Purple. That's an interesting name. Is he a purple dog?" While he spoke to the boy in a low tone, Gabe listened to his heart, checking his pulse and looking into his eyes.

"There's no such thing as a purple dog," the boy stated. "It's my favorite color."

Gabe chuckled and patted Bobby on the shoulder. "I'm sure you'll be playing with Marty soon." He spoke to the mother. "I think he'll be fine, but he may have a concussion and need to stay in the hospital overnight for observation."

Blinking, she swiped away the wetness on one cheek.

"I'll see that you're taken care of. Don't worry," Gabe assured her.

Seconds later the emergency medical techs arrived. They relieved Zoe and she stood. Her hands were a mess and one of the techs handed her a wet towel to clean them.

Gabe had been tender with Bobby, even able to distract him, which was a talent in itself. He showed promise at being a good father. Caring concern was every bit as evident in his interaction with the boy and mother as it had been during the night they had shared. Maybe it wouldn't be so hard to accept him as part of her and the baby's life. If he was truly serious about it. Her fear was that when reality set in he might change his mind. Right now, he was just being noble.

Gabe was busy giving the EMTs a report about what had happened when Zoe found her bag and headed to the nearest restroom to wash her hands. When she came out, Gabe stood nearby.

She checked her watch and shook her head. "I have to go. It's almost time for my plane. I have to get home."

He didn't look pleased with her putting him off once again. "I'll be in touch."

"Okay." She pulled a card from her purse and handed it to him. "My phone number is on it. 'Bye, Gabe."

CHAPTER TWO

TWO DAYS LATER Gabe was on his way out of surgery when his phone rang. "Hey, Mom."

"Hey yourself. I've not heard from you in weeks." His mother sounded eager to talk.

"I've been busy."

"Too busy to check in with your mother?" Her tone held a teasing note but there was also some scolding as well.

"I've been trying to wrap up things here. Planning a move at the same time has kept me tied up." Along with finding out he would soon be a father...

"I'm so proud of you and pleased you'll be moving closer. I don't see enough of you."

With his schedule, he couldn't promise it would be much different, but he did need to tell her about the baby. At least that would make her happy. "Mom, I'm glad you called. I've got some news."

"I hope it's good?"

"It is. I'm going to be a father." Even though he'd had a couple of days to adjust to the idea, the words still sounded strange.

"You are! I didn't even know you were seeing anyone!"

Gabe chuckled. His mother was as excited to hear the news as he had expected she would be. "I'm not really." He didn't want to get into it.

"Okay... Well, when is she due?"

"Sometime after the first of the year."

His mother shot back, "You don't know the exact date? Is it a boy or a girl?"

He really didn't know much. He and Zoe were going to have to really talk. Today. "I'll have to ask Zoe."

"I'm guessing she's the mother?" Curiosity filled her voice.

"Yes, her name is Zoe Avery."

"Where did you meet her?"

"At a professional meeting." He wasn't surprised his mother was full of questions.

"Gabe, I'm guessing this wasn't planned?" It sounded more like a question than a statement.

"It wasn't, but we're working all that out." His pager went off. He was needed in ICU. "Mom, I've got to go. I'll call you soon. I promise."

"Okay. I love you, son."

His mother might not have been around much, but he *had* known he was loved. His child would at least know Gabe cared, even if he couldn't be there for him all the time. He'd learned early from his mother that sacrifices were necessary to survive and succeed in a profession. That focus was important to get what you wanted. For him, that was to build a renowned liver-transplant program.

He checked on his patient in ICU the nurse had paged him about and increased the dosage of pain medicine, before giving instructions to his physician's assistant to notify him if there were additional issues. Then he headed to his office for some privacy. It was time he and Zoe had that overdue conversation. He just hoped she wouldn't try to evade it. They needed to discuss things whether she liked it or not.

She answered on the second ring.

"Zoe. It's Gabe. Please don't hang up."

"I wasn't going to." The soft voice that he'd know any-where as Zoe's sounded distracted.

"Uh… How're you doing?" He felt like a teen calling a girl for the first time. It mattered too much.

"I'm fine."

His chest tightened. She didn't sound like it. "Are you feeling okay?"

"I'm fine and so is the baby."

He was relieved to hear that. It amazed him how quickly she and his unborn child had become so important to him. "Uh, what's the baby's due date?" He'd been so shocked to learn she was pregnant he'd not thought to ask earlier.

"January twenty-second."

"My father was born in January." He shook his head. That was an odd statement. He'd not thought of that in a long time. "Do you know what it is yet?"

"No. I'll find out soon."

"You'll let me know as soon as you do?" Why should he want to hear so badly? How much time would he spend being a father anyway? More than Zoe apparently thought he should. Fatherhood wasn't what he'd planned for his life but now he had to adjust and adapt. He was determined to be the best father he could be.

"I will if you want me to."

He would like to tell his mother the sex. She would be so excited. Would start buying clothes. "Zoe, how did this happen?"

She tittered. "Why, Doctor, I thought you, of all people, understood the birds and the bees."

The Zoe with a sense of humor had returned. This was ground he was comfortable on. He huffed. "I don't mean the physical process. I thought you had things handled."

"I thought so too. I guess the pill failed." She sighed. "Or maybe the condom was bad. I don't know. I just know

I'm pregnant. I'm sorry, Gabe. I realize this isn't what you wanted."

It wasn't, but he could tell by her tone that she hadn't planned it either. "Maybe not, but I'll deal with it. Meet my responsibilities."

"This baby needn't ruin your life. I have things handled. I can raise it. I want to. There's no reason for you to change your lifestyle because of us. I know this wasn't in your life plan."

"You're not going to handle this alone. I'm here to help. I should help."

In the background, a woman called Zoe's name. Was that her mother?

"I'll be right there, Mom," Zoe said in an exasperated tone.

"Is everything okay?"

"Yes. And no." Zoe sounded bone weary. "Mom's Alzheimer's has really progressed. She's more confused these days. More demanding."

The faint sounds of Zoe's name being shouted again reached Gabe's ear.

"Sorry but I've got to go," Zoe said. "'Bye."

The click of them being disconnected was the last he heard.

The next day between surgeries he couldn't stop himself from texting her.

Is there a good time for me to call?

A few minutes later he received her reply.

Tonight. No later than ten-thirty my time. I have an early meeting in the morning.

Gabe typed back.

Will call at ten.

He needed to discuss his trip to her part of the world the next weekend. He would be looking for a house and wanted her to set aside some time to see him and discuss the baby's future.

His phone buzzed. He was needed in the emergency department. There had been a car accident. It turned out that his patient was a teenage girl who required surgery right away.

Hours later, Gabe left the operating room and checked his phone. He groaned. It was already after ten-thirty. Remorse filled him. He'd promised Zoe he would call her earlier. This was just another example of why he shouldn't have a family. He was so focused on his job. A wife and children deserved better than leftovers and afterthoughts. He would soon be a father. Where was he going to find the time? He had to show Zoe how serious he was about being a parent.

His child. Somehow that sounded weird and right at the same time.

Regardless of the time, he needed to talk to Zoe, even if just to make plans for the weekend.

She answered on the first ring. "Hello." The word was said quietly as if he had woken her.

He remembered her voice sounding like that the night they had spent together. "It's Gabe."

"I know."

Was that because of caller ID or because she recognized his voice? He hoped the latter. Now that he was actually speaking to her, he was a little unsure. "I'm sorry I'm late calling. I didn't think you'd be asleep yet. There was an emergency and time got away from me. How're you doing?" he finally asked.

"Fair, all things considered."

"Has something happened to the baby?" Gabe's middle clinched at the thought. He was surprised at how quickly his mind had gone that direction.

"No. The baby is fine. The doctor said today it measures just right. Heartbeat is strong."

An odd feeling washed over him. He was relieved to hear it. "Was everything all right with your mom after last night?"

"Yeah, she was just confused. She gets more anxious and demanding these days. She's asleep now."

"That must be stressful." He couldn't imagine what he'd do with his job demands if his mother required his attention like Zoe's did.

"I don't wish this disease on anyone."

Gabe had heard Alzheimer's was difficult to deal with, but this was the first time he'd known someone facing it daily. "Do you have any help?"

"Not really. My sister lives about four hours away and travels for work, so she can't come often." There was a pause, and then she asked, "Do you happen to know how the boy from Chicago is doing? His mother was beside herself."

"She was, but she was much better after she knew Bobby was going to be all right and they had a place to stay for the night. I spoke to her the other day and Bobby is doing just great."

"You called her?"

Gabe grinned. "Don't sound so surprised. I did. I like to keep track of my patients. She said if it weren't for the stitches in his head she wouldn't even know anything had happened."

"Good. I'm glad to hear it. You were good with him. Both as a doctor and a person."

"Thanks. I like to see that my patients get complete care. You weren't half-bad yourself. Using the diaper to stop the blood flow was quick thinking."

"It's my turn to say thanks."

The self-assured Zoe had returned. Smiling to himself, he got down to business. "I wanted to let you know I'll be in town this weekend, looking for a place to live. I'd like to see you. Discuss things without being interrupted."

"Look, Gabe, I appreciate what you're trying to do, really I do. But you don't need to feel obligated. I'm fine. I can take care of the baby."

His blood ran hot. Why did she keep pushing him away when he was offering to help? Did she expect he'd be satisfied with a phone call here and there and a few school pictures? It was time to make himself clear. "Zoe, I have every intention of being an active parent in my child's life. You're not going to push me out of it. I'll gladly handle my share of the expenses. I not only want to be involved, I *will* be involved. Let's try to keep this between us and not drag others into the situation."

Silence lay heavy between them.

She must have gotten his less-than-subtle hint about hiring a lawyer. He didn't want to go there but he would if he had to. Growing up without a father hadn't been fun. At baseball games there hadn't been a man in the stands cheering him on or coaching on the sidelines. When he'd liked his first girl and she had wanted nothing to do with him, there had been no man to listen and offer advice based on experience. His mother had tried but it just hadn't been the same. Those memories only made him all the more determined to be a present father to his child. It was his child, his responsibility.

After his and Zoe's night together, he'd like to believe

they had parted friends, albeit uncomfortable ones, but civil nonetheless. He wanted to build on that. He had no interest in angering Zoe, so he volunteered in a conciliatory tone, "I'll be looking at houses most of the day on Saturday, so how about having dinner with me that evening?"

"I can't. I don't have anyone to watch Mother."

"Then I'll pick up something and bring it to your place. I'd really like for us to talk about this." He wasn't letting Zoe run from him forever. He saw another call was coming in. He'd have to get it. "The floor is paging me. I'll be in touch on Saturday."

By Wednesday, Zoe had red-rimmed eyes, a runny nose and was sneezing.

"Of all the times to get a head cold," she murmured as she headed down the hall of one of the local hospitals to see a patient. She already had her hands full with life and her job, and to feel awful was almost more than she could take. Since Gabe's call, she was still trying to sort out her thoughts and feelings.

The reality of him moving to the area, of seeing him on a regular basis was slowly seeping in. Against her better judgment she looked forward to seeing him again. That was a road she needed to close but how could she when their lives were becoming more intertwined, both personally and professionally? Her life was changing so fast she was racing to catch up. What more could happen?

She sanitized her hands using the liquid in the container by the patient's door and pulled out a mask from the box on the shelf nearby. Mr. Luther was her most difficult patient but one her heart went out to. Why, she didn't know. He didn't make it easy. It could be Mr. Luther was the father figure she was missing in her life or that he just didn't have anyone else. He reminded her of a bad-tempered grandfather who hid his huge soft spot well.

For some reason she was the one person he would listen to. Maybe he sensed she liked him despite his rough outer shell. Regardless, she was determined to do whatever she could to help him.

Knocking on the hospital door, she waited until she heard the gruff "Yeah."

She took a deep breath to fortify herself for what was coming. Pushing the door open, Zoe entered the dark room where the TV was blaring. The sixty-four-year-old man who sat in a chair beside the bed didn't even look her way as she entered.

He'd been in and out of the hospital for months with advancing inflammation of the liver caused by hepatitis C. Because of it he had a yellow tint to his skin and eyes and ongoing nausea and fatigue. It didn't look like he would have any improvement without a transplant. She hoped that Gabe might help her there. When the time was right she'd ask him. With any luck, Mr. Luther would be transferred to Gabe's care at National Hospital and listed for a transplant.

"Hello, Mr. Luther. How're you doing this morning?"

"You know as well as I do how I'm doing."

She might but she wouldn't let him get away with ignoring her. "Do you mind if we turn the TV down?"

"I do but I guess you'll do it anyway."

Zoe grinned as she found the remote and lowered the volume. She'd learned long ago that his bark was worse than his bite. "I need to give you a listen and have you sign a couple of forms so I have permission to look at your chart."

"The others here have already listened to me today."

"You know how this works by now. I have to do my own listening and looking at lab results if I'm going to help you get better. I'm your advocate. I don't work for the hospital. I work for you. I'm here to help you."

"Aw, go ahead. You will anyway."

Zoe stepped to him. Pulling her stethoscope out of her pocket and placing the ends in her ears, she proceeded to listen to his heart. It sounded steady and strong, which pleased her. She then listened to his lungs and checked his pulse rate. Removing her small penlight from her lab coat pocket, she said, "I need to look in your eyes."

"I was afraid of that." Mr. Luther lifted his face to her.

She pointed the light in his eyes. What she found there she wasn't as happy with. The whites still weren't clear.

"Well? Will I be getting out of here soon?"

"That's not for me to say. Your doctor here makes those decisions. But I will be in touch. If I don't see you here next week, I'll be calling you at home to check on you." She didn't have to keep such close tabs on him, but as far as she knew, there was no one else to do it. Zoe placed her hand on his shoulder. "Please do what they say, Mr. Luther."

He grunted. "Always do."

She looked back at him as she went out the door. He was going to need a liver transplant much sooner than the doctors had originally estimated.

As she traveled to different hospitals to check on other patients and completed paperwork in her office over the next few days, she continued to search for reasons not to see Gabe while he was in town. The longer she could put him off, the better. Dealing with him was the last thing she needed at this point in her emotionally and physically overloaded life.

Preparing for her baby's birth, dealing with her mother's rapidly deteriorating condition and now the urgent need to get Mr. Luther on the fast track for a liver transplant... If only Gabe would stop pressuring her to make decisions about her baby's future, decisions that could wait until closer to the due date. If Gabe sincerely wanted to help her, maybe she could convince him to give her those precious three months before her baby was born to deal with her other problems by priority. Would he understand her genuine need for time and distance? Or would he be self-centered, accusing her of trying to push him out of the baby's life?

On Saturday afternoon, her mother had gone to her room for a nap and Zoe was trying to get some much-needed rest on the sofa. The cold was taking its toll on her. She'd just closed her eyes when the phone rang. Anticipation zinged through her. Would it be Gabe?

"Hey," he said when she answered, not giving his name. It wasn't necessary. Zoe would have known his voice anywhere. "Have you changed your mind about going out to dinner?"

"No." Even to her own ears she didn't sound welcoming, yet blood whipped through her veins at the mere fact she was speaking to Gabe.

"You sound awful. What's wrong?"

"I woke with a cold the other morning."

"Are you taking care of it? Getting enough rest?" His concern somehow made her feel better. She liked knowing Gabe cared about her, even if it was just because of the baby.

"Yes. I'm just tired."

"Then I'll pick up dinner. Bring it to you. What's your address?"

She gave it to him.

"I'll see you in about an hour and a half. 'Bye."

Knowing she was about to see Gabe again caused her stomach to flutter. Despite feeling bad, she still rushed around, putting her apartment in order in anticipation of his visit. Her life was already a tightrope and Gabe was tying complicated knots in it as well. With one more tiny twist she might snap.

Zoe finally settled on the sofa to wait for him. She hadn't missed his poorly veiled threat about getting a lawyer involved if she didn't talk to him. The nervous waves in her stomach crashed harder, despite him brushing off his threat with a dinner offer. He'd made it plain he didn't want a wife and children the night they had been together. His declaration of lifelong bachelorhood over five months ago contradicted his current insistence on being involved with their child. How long would his sense of obligation last? Until "his" child started making demands on his time? Would he still be sharing parental duties when they started to interfere with his career? Maybe he didn't mind being a father as much as he hated the thought of being a husband. If that was the case, she was left with the conclusion he would never marry her.

That hurt. It shouldn't, but it did.

She had no doubt Gabe wouldn't consider marriage as a practical solution to their situation. In the unlikely event he did, she would say no. Being wanted because she was the mother of his child wasn't good enough. When she married it would be for love. Her hand went to her middle. Right now, her focus would be on the baby. She wasn't going to let Gabe continue making immediate demands that would needlessly confuse her life further.

The door buzzer woke Zoe. Panic filled her. She'd had every intention of having time to apply some makeup and fix her hair before Gabe arrived. She stopped in front of a mirror on the way to the door and pushed at her hair, creating some order, before she checked the peephole, getting a distorted view of Gabe. Even then he looked amazing. Why couldn't he be everything she *didn't* want in a man?

Zoe unlocked and opened the door. Gabe had two large white bags in his hands and one small brown one. She'd never seen him casually dressed. The white-collared shirt he wore rolled up his forearms set off his dark hair and California tan. Jeans hugged his slim hips and loafers covered his feet. He could be a model for a men's cologne ad. He took her breath away.

For seconds, they just looked at each other. He broke the silence. "May I come in?"

"Yes." Zoe pushed the door wider.

Gabe entered, looked around, then headed toward the kitchen table, where he set the bags down. "You sit down and rest. I'll get things on the table. Just tell me where they are."

Zoe closed the door and followed more slowly. Her apartment went from small to tiny with Gabe in it. She needed to get a grip on her attraction to him or she would lose control of the situation.

Her mother joined them, looking from Gabe and back to her, perplexed.

Zoe put a reassuring hand on her mother's arm. "Mom, I want you to meet a friend of mine, Gabe Marks."

"Friend" might be stretching their actual relationship, but she didn't want to explain more.

Gabe came around the table with a smile on his face. "Mrs. Avery, it's a pleasure to meet you."

Her mother smiled. "Hello."

"I brought you some dinner. I hope you're hungry." He pulled a chair out from under the table and held it for her.

"Thank you. I am." Her smile broadened as she sat.

Zoe sank into a chair.

Gabe returned to the bags, continuing to remove cartons. "Zoe, I hate it, but I forgot drinks."

How like him to take control and look comfortable doing it. "I have iced tea made."

"Sounds great." He looked at her mother and smiled. "That work for you too, Mrs. Avery?"

Her mother grinned, an endearing expression Zoe hadn't seen in some time, and nodded to Gabe. The devil was charming her mother out of her fog.

Zoe stood.

"I said I'd get things." He waved her down and headed into the kitchen. "Just tell me where they are. Plates? Silverware?"

"I don't feel that bad." Zoe joined him. Gabe took her by the arm and gently led her back to her chair.

Her body trembled at his touch. She sat, forcing him to release her. If he had noticed her hypersensitive reaction to him, he didn't show it, much to her relief. She had to somehow smother her physical desire for him. She couldn't spend the rest of her life fighting it and hiding it from him.

"You may not feel very bad at the moment, but you don't need to exert yourself any more than absolutely necessary. You don't want to get worse." His tone said he'd accept no argument.

Zoe huffed then gave him directions to which cabinet and drawer he needed. He soon had the table set and was heading into the kitchen again.

"Glasses?"

"Cabinet next to the refrigerator."

After the chinking of ice dropping into glasses, Gabe brought two drinks to the table and returned to get the other. He took the seat at the head of the table. For some reason that held significance. As if he was taking on more importance in her life than she wanted.

"Who are you?" her mother asked. In a different situation Zoe might have thought it was funny. Her mother might be as overwhelmed by Gabe as Zoe was, but in this instance she was afraid her mother just didn't remember.

Gabe answered before Zoe had a chance to. "I'm Gabe."

"Oh, yeah, that's right."

He didn't miss a beat and started opening containers. "Would you like a piece of fried chicken, Mrs. Avery?"

"Yes, that would be nice."

Gabe picked up her plate and placed a piece on it. "How about potatoes, green beans and a roll?"

"Please."

Gabe finished serving her plate and put it in front of her. "Mrs. Avery, did Zoe tell you that I'm moving to the area?"

She looked at Zoe. "No, she didn't. You'll like it here. Henry and I moved here when we were newlyweds."

"So you've lived around here for a long time," Gabe said as he scooped food onto another plate.

Zoe watched her mother become dreamy-eyed as memories surfaced. "We had the best time together."

That was until Zoe's father had left and never returned. In her mother's illness she only remembered the good times, but Zoe clearly recalled the hurt and devastation her father had left behind. She never wanted to live through that again.

"I'm sure you did." Gabe smiled at her then opened the brown bag. He looked at Zoe. "I forgot. I made a special stop for you." He pulled out a plastic container of liquid. "Chicken soup. Let me get you a bowl and spoon." Before she could say anything, he was on his way back to the kitchen. When he returned, he poured the soup in the bowl and placed it and the spoon in front of her.

He'd made a stop just for her? When had someone last made her feel so special? The soup smelled heavenly. She met Gabe's expectant expression. "Thanks. This hits the spot."

"Who're you?" her mother asked.

Zoe couldn't help but chuckle this time. She was asking herself the same thing. Was there another man like him? If there was, she'd never met him.

"I'm Gabe."

"That's right. Did you know that Zoe's having a baby?" She looked at Zoe.

Gabe looked at her as well. "Yes, ma'am, I see that."

"She'll be a good mother. She's a nurse, you know." Her mother's attention returned to her food.

"I do know." He continued to watch Zoe. "I also think she'll be a good mother."

"Are you Zoe's boyfriend?"

"Mom!"

Gabe's eyes questioned her as if asking permission to answer. Was he wondering how much her mother knew? It was time to come clean. "Mom, Gabe is the baby's father."

Her mother studied him closely. "You will get married." That wasn't a question but a statement.

Embarrassment flooded Zoe. She couldn't even look at Gabe. "Mom! You can't go around telling men to marry me."

Her mother ignored her and went back to eating. "This is good," she said, not missing a beat. As if she hadn't created a cloud of tension in the room.

It took a few minutes for Zoe to find the courage to even glance at Gabe. He seemed to have taken the exchange in his stride.

After their meal Zoe settled her mother in her room to watch TV and returned to find Gabe had cleaned up the table. "I'm sorry about that. I don't expect you to marry me. I've never thought you should."

"Don't worry about it," he said in an even tone. "I put some coffee on. I hope you don't mind. It's been a long day." He hung the washcloth up.

"I'm not surprised. You pretty much came in and made yourself at home." She hadn't meant to sound irritated, even though she was…a little.

A shocked look came over his face. "I'm sorry. That

wasn't my intent. I hadn't eaten since early this morning, having looked at houses all day. Plus, I knew you didn't feel well and I guess I just got carried away."

Was she being too sensitive? He had her so out of sorts she'd not even thought about him, his needs. This situation couldn't be any easier on him than it was on her. If she met him halfway then maybe it would be better. She could at least try. "Why don't you go have a seat in the living room and I'll bring you a cup of coffee. How do you like it?"

"Black is fine."

With coffee in hand, she found Gabe sitting on the sofa, legs stretched out with his head back and his eyes closed. Was he asleep? Why did it seem so natural to have him in her home?

He quickly straightened when she set the mug on the table closest to him. He ran his hands through his wavy hair. "Thanks. I'd rather do two transplants back-to-back than look at houses all day."

She settled in the chair facing him.

Gabe took a sip of his coffee.

"Did you find a place?" Was it nearby? Could she handle him being so close?

"I did. It's out in Vernon Landing."

Zoe breathed a sigh of relief. It wasn't as local as she'd feared. The traffic alone would make him think twice before he just showed up. She wouldn't allow that anyway. He was right—they needed to talk. They needed to at least agree on visitation guidelines before the baby was born.

"I'm glad you found something." She couldn't help but ask, "When will you be moving in?"

"Two weeks."

Her heart did a thump-bump. "That soon."

"Yeah. I'm to start my new position on the first of the month."

Zoe had hoped for more time to adjust to the idea of him living nearby.

"I know this is going to be an adjustment," he remarked as though he could read her mind. "Neither one of us planned how things have turned out."

That was an understatement if Zoe had ever heard one. Her hand went to her belly.

"Zoe."

She looked at him.

"I have no intention of taking the baby away from you. All I want is to be in his life. See him or her occasionally. Do my share financially."

That declaration did make her feel better. He sounded sincere, not threatening. Having him help financially would be nice, especially since her mother was going to require ever more costly care as time went on. However, she wouldn't let Gabe think for a moment he could do as he pleased where the baby was concerned. "You know, you can't just show up here unannounced."

He put his mug down, placing his arms on his knees with hands clasped between them, and leaned toward her. "I would never do that."

"We're going to have to set rules and guidelines. I'll be raising him or her." How matter-of-fact she sounded pleased her. *She* was in control of this discussion.

"Agreed. But big decisions like schools, medical care, moving out of town should be discussed with me." Gabe's dark expression warned of his unwillingness to negotiate.

"Moving?" That he had given the future that much thought startled her. She was going to have to make a change of living space soon.

His expression didn't waver. "I won't allow you to take him or her to the other side of the country to where it makes it hard to be a part of their life."

She appreciated his rights as a father, but she wasn't

going to build her world around his wants. She started to say as much but he cut her off. "When I get settled, why don't I get a lawyer to draw up an agreement? That way we'll both know where we stand. You can make a list and I will too. Then we can compare and come to a satisfactory compromise."

Zoe considered his suggestion with care. She had intended to tell him his role in their child's life wasn't to dictate how she would raise her child, but doing so would result in arguing about it. "All right. I can do that."

Gabe stood. "Then I'd better go. I have a bit of a drive to the hotel."

Zoe rose too and followed him to the door. "Uh, Gabe, before you go, could I ask you about something?"

He looked at her. "Sure."

"I hate to ask you this before you even started your new job, but I have a patient, Mr. Luther. He's medically fragile and his liver is failing. He could really use your expertise. He can be a difficult patient but he's getting sicker and sicker…" She'd had other patients sicker than Mr. Luther, so why was she so concerned about him? He would end up being like the other men in her life and just pass through—but she still wanted the best for him.

"Email me his file and I'll have a look."

"Thank you." Why did she believe Gabe would make it all right? It would be so easy to lean on him in her professional life as well as her personal one. But could she count on him always being there?

His gaze met hers, held. Heat built in her. That same effect he'd had on her during their night together was there, curling around her, tugging her closer to him. Gabe's hand gently brushed a thread of hair away from her cheek. "You're welcome. I should go. Take care of yourself. Please tell your mother I said 'bye. See you soon."

That sounded like a promise. Zoe couldn't help but wish

for more even as she told herself that was the last thing she needed. She closed the door behind him. Something about Gabe made her want to ask him to stay longer. Yet she knew those feelings, if she acted on them, would only make matters worse.

CHAPTER THREE

GABE STEPPED INTO an empty conference room at the hospital and tapped Zoe's number on his phone for the second time that day. A couple of days had passed before he'd allowed himself to call her, convincing himself he should check on her, the baby. He could have texted, but for some inexplicable reason he was eager to hear Zoe's voice.

She'd sent the files as he had requested. He was still reviewing them, but he'd already decided to examine Mr. Luther as soon as possible. Why hadn't Zoe at least called or texted him about the patient she was so concerned about?

After a number of rings there was still no answer. What was going on with her? Had something happened to the baby? To Zoe? Her mother?

He was thousands of miles away with no way of knowing. Why didn't Zoe answer? He would try her one more time. If she didn't pick up he'd call the police and have them stop by her place. Gabe touched the green icon and listened to three rings.

On the fourth a breathless voice said, "Hello?"

Relief flooded him, the tension ebbing away from his shoulders. "Zoe, I've been calling you all day."

"Gabe, I don't need this today."

"What's wrong?"

There was an exasperated sound on the other end, and

then Zoe said, "Mother decided to cook bacon. She left the pan on the burner. The kitchen caught fire. I'm at the hospital right now."

His gut felt like someone had it in their fist and was twisting it. "Is she all right? Are you?"

"They're treating her for smoke inhalation. She'll be in the hospital at least overnight. The fire alarm went off and one of the neighbors called the fire department. They got there quickly or it could have been much worse." She paused. "I'm fine and the baby is too."

He said gently, "It may be time to find your mother a place where she'll have full-time care."

"I know, but that's costly. I can't afford an apartment and pay for a place for her to stay. Her insurance doesn't kick in until she is fifty-nine and a half. That's another seven months. I'll just have to figure something out until then. The doctor has just come in. I have to go. 'Bye."

"'Bye." He spoke into silence.

Unable to stand not knowing what was going on any longer, Gabe took the first opportunity he had and called again around midmorning the next day. He tapped his pen against his desk in his apprehension about how she would react to his suggestion that she come and live with him. Zoe answered on the first ring.

"How're things today?" he asked.

"Better." She sounded tired.

He wished he was there to hold her. Whoa—that wasn't a thought he should be having, or the type of relationship they had. "That's good to hear. I'm concerned about you. Are you taking care of yourself?"

"I told you—the baby's fine," she informed him, as if he hadn't just asked about her welfare.

Did she think he was only concerned about the baby and not her? "I want to know about you as well. Have you been able to make some plans?" Would she consider his idea? For some reason it really mattered to him that she accept his plan.

"A few. The doctor said Mom could stay in the hospital a week. That'll give me time to look for an assisted-living home for her. I don't want her to make any unnecessary moves. She's already confused enough."

Strength and determination had returned to Zoe's voice. "Can you go back to your apartment?"

"No. It's so damaged it's uninhabitable. I'll have to find a new place."

This was his opening to offer his solution. "I have something I want you to consider and I want you to hear it out before you say anything. Right now, your most urgent problem is twofold: finding somewhere your mother will be safe and that has adequate full-time care, *and* somewhere for you to live. Let me help."

"Gabe, I'm not taking money." She sounded iron-rod strong. "I can handle things on my own."

"Please hear me out." Why wouldn't she let him help her? Zoe's independence would get her into trouble one day. "I'm sure you can, but if you'll listen, I think you might find my plan practical and helpful."

She huffed then said, "Okay. What do you think I should do?"

"I think you need to move in with me."

"What!"

He jerked the phone away from his ear.

She came close to yelling, "That's not going to happen. No way."

Gabe interrupted, using his giving-order-in-the-OR voice. "Just listen. You need to find a place for your mother. Money is an issue. If you stay at my house, where I have plenty of room, you'd be able to pay for a place for her while you wait for her insurance to start."

"Thank you, but I don't think so." Her words sounded as though they were coming through clenched teeth.

"Why not?" He'd offered a practical solution. Couldn't she see that?

"Because you don't need to be involved in my problems, my private life." She sounded as if he should have known that.

"If it'll make you feel any better, I'm interested in seeing that my child comes into the world with a mother who hasn't been sleeping on a couch in someone's living room. Who isn't stressed out over finances. It'll just be for a few months. We'd only be housemates. You can pay rent if you like."

"I appreciate your offer, but I don't think it would work." Her voice had calmed, but her resolve was loud and clear.

What was that supposed to mean? It was a practical solution. "Just think about it."

"I have to go. Mother's calling me. Her nurse has just come in."

Silence filled his ear. He wasn't surprised that she'd shot the idea down and ended the call. If nothing else, he'd learned Zoe was stubborn.

Zoe resisted the impulse to kick something. How dared Gabe think that she would move in with him? She didn't even know him. Just because she was having his child, it didn't mean he had any say over her life.

Up until a week ago they hadn't really talked, and even then all they'd done was agree to make lists of what they wanted. And have a lawyer make it legal. She mustn't forget that part of his idea. She should have rejected his idea outright and told him what he could and could not do when it came to his rights. Instead she'd meekly agreed to avoid an argument.

Now he was trying to move her around like a pawn on a chessboard. She wasn't having it. Taking care of her mother, her baby and herself was her job, her decisions to make. She didn't need or want him butting into her life anytime he pleased. Besides, if she started letting him make major decisions about her life, what would she do when he got tired of playing daddy or didn't have time for her when the next crisis cropped up? One thing she had learned was that she must be careful who she depended on.

Two days later Zoe wasn't feeling nearly as confident. Since she couldn't return to her apartment, her renter's insurance was paying for a hotel room until she found a place to live or for fourteen days, whichever came first. Her priority over the weekend had been to locate a place for her mother to live. That had turned out to be more difficult than anticipated.

She'd visited every assisted-care facility in the immediate area. Responsibility weighed heavily on her about having to put her mother in a home. She had found one that would be suitable, but it was way beyond her budget. Guilt squeezed her heart.

Between searching for facilities for her mother and her full-time job, there hadn't yet been time to look for a place for herself. Her apartment manager told her that there wasn't an empty apartment available in the complex. Since her lease was almost up, Zoe would have to look elsewhere. Fourteen days in which to see to her mother's needs and find a new home for herself, not to mention getting packed to move. There simply wasn't enough time. She was almost at her wits' end.

Her workload was heavy, but she'd managed to squeeze in checking on Mr. Luther. He'd been discharged from the hospital, where he'd been treated for stomach pain and fatigue. These were just symptoms of a larger issue that wouldn't get better without a transplant. It was time he be admitted to National Hospital for a transplant workup. Thankfully he wasn't so sick he couldn't go home until that time, but that wouldn't be the case for much longer. When she could think straight again she must talk to Gabe about him.

That night at the hotel while Zoe sat eating takeout food, her phone rang. It was Gabe. She hated to admit it, but his unwelcomed suggestion was starting to look like the only answer. "Hello."

"It's Gabe." He sounded unsure. Was he afraid of her reaction after his last call?

"Hi." She was so tired and disheartened she was glad to have someone to talk to, and Gabe was a good listener.

"How're things going?"

She loved the deep timbre of his voice. There was something reassuring about it. "They could be better." Zoe sounded as down as she felt. She refused to show weakness. Appearing needy wouldn't help her either. Gabe was already making plans regarding the baby she'd not counted on.

"Your mother?"

"She's actually recovering well." For that Zoe was grateful.

"What, then?"

"I've been out looking at homes for her." Her hand cradled her baby bump. The weight of her responsibilities was growing.

"And?"

"They were awful. I can't stand the idea of putting Mother in one. I hate myself for having to do it." Why was she spilling all of this to him? What was it about Gabe that made her want to lean on him? Their relationship was nothing like that, yet she was becoming more deeply involved with him each time they talked.

"What's happening with your mother isn't your fault. You know for her health and safety she needs to be in professional care where she'll be safe and well cared for. What occurred a few days ago proves it. You're not abandoning her. You're doing it because you love her."

His voice was gentle and reassuring, washing over her tight nerves like a warm balm. "Thanks for saying that. I just wish it wasn't necessary."

"You didn't find any place you liked?"

"I found the better of the evils." If only she had the money to put her mother there. Even if she emptied her savings she'd still be short. It was just as well there was no room available. She'd have to settle on one of the other places that weren't as nice as Shorecliffs House.

"So, will you move her in when she's able to leave the hospital?"

"Yes. I'm making arrangements tomorrow."

"I'm glad you found a place for her. Any luck on a new apartment for you?"

"I haven't had time to worry about that. I'll be good in the hotel for at least a few more days. I have to see what I can salvage out of the apartment. I know the living-room furniture will have to go. It smells too much like smoke. I can keep the tables and such, but everything has to be wiped down and packed up." It wasn't a job she was looking forward to, even if she would just be overseeing things.

"You'll have some help with that?" Concern filled his voice.

She pushed pillows behind her and leaned back against the headboard. "The insurance company has a crew coming in. I just have to find some place to put what's salvageable, like another apartment."

"I'm sorry this happened."

She could imagine him pulling her into a hug. "Me too,

but at least it made me face the inevitable. Mom needs more help than I can give her."

"Tough way to figure that out." Sincere sympathy surrounded his words.

"You're not kidding." Why was it so easy to talk to Gabe? She should be putting distance between them, not making him a confidant.

There was quiet on the line before he said, "Have you thought about my offer?"

She'd suspected that question would come up before the call ended. "Gabe, I'm not living with you."

"The invitation remains open if you change your mind. I'll be moving your way on Friday. I hate it but I've gotta go. Surgery is paging me. 'Bye."

Suddenly Zoe felt utterly alone. He seemed to always be rushing off somewhere. If only Gabe could have talked to her longer. She needed his logical reasoning because she hated the idea of her mother going into a care home. There was no one else to lean on. Her sister was out of the country. Zoe hadn't even been able to get in touch with her to tell her about the fire. Zoe had friends, but they had become rather distant since she'd had to spend so much time with her mother. Now that she needed someone, Gabe was filling that spot. It was odd. They knew so little about each other, yet they seemed to click.

She ran her hands over her belly. They certainly had clicked that one night. He'd been easy to be around then and he was now. Too easy.

Zoe stuffed her leftover meal into the paper bag and threw it in the garbage. Going back to bed, she slid between the bedsheets. Curling into a ball as she hugged a pillow to her, she let the tears she'd held in check flow. What would it be like to have strong, sure arms around her? Comforting arms? Someone to share her pain with?

That was what she'd always dreamed of. Gabe's face popped into her mind. She couldn't depend on him. He didn't want a wife and family. Just like her ex-fiancé and her father. She couldn't let her heart be hurt again like he had so easily done. She had to wait for the right man to give her heart to. The one who wanted the same things out of life that she did.

She did have her baby. Zoe smiled. Another person to take care of but she was looking forward to it. Would her child have Gabe's big blue eyes and dark hair? Or look more like her? In a few short months she would know. Hold him or her in her arms. Out of all this darkness there would be a shining star. With a slight smile on her lips, Zoe fell into an exhausted sleep.

The next afternoon she received a call from Shorecliffs House, the assisted-living home she couldn't afford. The administrator said they had a room opening after all. Before the woman had hardly finished, Zoe had said she would take it. When the conversation was over Zoe put her head against the wall and tapped it a few times. She knew what she had to do. The only way she could afford it was by moving in with Gabe until her mother's insurance would cover the cost.

Backing down and agreeing to Gabe's plan put her in a vulnerable position. There must be ground rules. Above all else they would not be sharing a bed. Ever. That rule couldn't be broken regardless of how tempting it might be.

With a lump in her throat she worked to swallow, Zoe pushed Gabe's phone number. He didn't answer, so she left a message. "Please call me."

A few hours later, while working at her old apartment, her phone rang. With shaking hands and banging heart, she said, "Hello?"

"Hey, what's going on?" He sounded distracted.

"That proposition you made about me renting a room from you—did you really mean it?"

"Yeah, I really mean it. Wouldn't have offered if I didn't." He seemed totally focused on their conversation now.

"It looks like I'm going to need to take you up on a room. But there have to be some rules."

"Such as?"

"I pay rent. I have my own room. I'm strictly a room-mate. I'll only stay until my mother's insurance starts. We lead our own lives without reporting in to each other."

"Okay." He drew the word out. "Do you mind if I ask what changed your mind?"

"The home I wanted to put Mom in had an opening. I had to jump at the chance when they called. Having a roommate is the only way I can afford it. I don't have time to look for one, so…"

"I see." By his tone he did.

"The arrangement will only be temporary. I'll be out in six months, tops. I'll have found my own place by then." Hers and the baby's.

"I don't have a problem with that. My house is plenty big enough for us both. My bedroom is on one side of the house while the other two bedrooms are on the other. We might meet in the kitchen occasionally.

"With my new position, I'll be super-busy, so I probably won't be around much. I'll be moving in on Friday. Why don't you let me make the arrangements for the movers to pick up your furniture?"

"I don't really have much. Everything I own smells like smoke. The insurance had to give me money for clothes. I'm at the apartment, boxing up family pictures and such now. I'll put whatever I decide I don't need in storage. I think my bedroom suite and Mom's should be all right but the mattresses may have to go. Anyway, I don't need to bore you with all that. I'll figure it all out and get back to you."

"Zoe, I already have my movers coming. You have enough going on. Let them take care of moving your stuff as well."

"You've got your hands full with your own move. I'll take care of mine." She had to start setting boundaries now. This she would do for herself. At least she could feel in control of one area of her life.

He huffed. "If that's the way you want it. Let me know when you're ready to move in and I'll make sure you can get into the house."

Someone in the background called his name. To them he said, "Yeah, I'll be right there. I need to do it myself." He spoke to her again. "I've got a case that needs my attention, so I've got to go. Take care of yourself."

Gabe didn't like the thought of Zoe handling her own moving arrangements or of her lifting boxes, but with her attitude, he wouldn't be doing himself any favors by pushing her further. He decided to keep his distance, trying not to think about what she was doing and why. He made a point of not calling her, even though he was anxious to know how she was doing.

Had her mother's move gone well? This personal interest in Zoe perplexed him. It wasn't like him. He put it down to the fact that she was the mother of his child. And he genuinely liked her. If he didn't hear from her soon he'd be forced to call her. On Thursday evening, he flew to Richmond and resisted the urge to try to see Zoe. If he hadn't heard from her by Friday evening he would call.

Early the next day he was standing on the porch of his new home, waiting for the movers to show up. He didn't have many belongings, had never cared much about what his home looked like as long as it was comfortable. With

his more-gone-than-home lifestyle, he had never felt the
need to decorate his places.

Apartments had always been where he'd lived as an
adult, but with a child coming, a house had seemed like
the right thing to buy. A boy needed a backyard. Or a girl.
The idea of having a place for his son or daughter to play
like he'd had appealed. He may not have had a father but
he'd had a good childhood. He looked around him at the
tree-lined street with the sidewalk running along it and the
other houses with their green lawns and shook his head. A
subdivision wasn't where he'd ever dreamed he'd be living.

Next thing he knew he'd be driving a minivan. The
very idea made him huff. Yet he'd made a step in that direction today. He had sold his sports car and picked up his
new four-door sedan. His argument to himself was that
he was being practical, because it would be easier to get
a car seat in and out of.

A moving van pulled into his drive. The large truck
held his meager belongings—bedroom suite, kitchen table,
sofa, boxed kitchen items and household goods. There
would be a large amount of space in the house sitting
empty. Maybe what he needed to do was hire an interior
decorator to come in and suggest what he needed to buy.

A few hours later the movers had left, and he was searching through a box for the coffee maker when his phone
rang. His heart beat faster. It was Zoe. "Hey."

"I just wanted to let you know that I'm not going to
move in until Sunday."

He was both disappointed and surprised. "Oh, okay.
Why not earlier?"

"I've had to deal with Mother. And the guys can't help
me until Sunday afternoon. I've spent most of the morning organizing what needs to go into storage and pack-
ing up the rest."

"Guys?" What guys was she talking about? She wouldn't

let him help her; instead, she'd chosen to ask some other men. There was a pang in his chest he didn't want to examine closely.

"Some friends from work," came her offhanded answer.

"It sounds like you have everything in hand." Could she hear the testiness he felt?

"Why I'm calling is to see if it's all right for me to come over and see what my room looks like. I need to decide what to bring and what to store."

His ego took another hit. She was only interested in seeing the house, not him. It occurred to him he was taking this all too personally because he was operating on the assumption they were more than merely accidental parents. Which they weren't, so why was he feeling this way? He had to get control of his imagination, be ruthlessly realistic about the foundation of their relationship. Starting now. "Sure. That'll be fine."

"How much longer do you think your movers will be? I don't want to get in their way."

She was all business. He could be that as well. "They left hours ago, so you're welcome anytime."

"Great. Please text me your address. I'll see you later." She hung up.

Gabe lost track of the number of times he'd checked his watch since Zoe had called. It amazed him how excited he was at the thought of seeing her again. The doorbell finally rang as he finished unpacking the last box in his bedroom.

He wiped his hands on his jeans and hurried to the front of the house. Through the pane glass of the door he could see Zoe. His heart beat faster. She was as amazing as he remembered. Her head was moving one way then another as if she was taking everything in. Pulling the door open wide, he stepped back and said in a welcoming manner, "Come in."

Zoe gave him a slight smile. "Hi. I like your house. It's...big."

He wasn't sure how to take that statement. Was she being complimentary or expressing relief they wouldn't be living in close proximity? Or both?

With a tentative step, Zoe entered Gabe's new home. Stepping into his living space symbolized how drastically her life was changing. It wasn't an unpleasant feeling, just one of uncertainty. As if she'd been forced to open a door without knowing what lay behind it.

It was a new redbrick home in an exclusive neighborhood that she'd only driven through a couple of times. She was a little surprised he'd chosen the area and such a large house. This was a subdivision of family homes, not where single men tended to live. Gabe didn't impress her as a spacious-home kind of person. So why had he decided on this one?

It did have one appealing advantage, though. It was large enough they would most likely have little or no contact while she resided here. That was what she wanted. To get through the next few months then move on. Or at least that was what she was going to keep telling herself.

She ran her fingertips over the smooth wooden door with its beautiful glass panels and large oval in the middle. A hardwood floor gleamed in the shaft of afternoon sun flowing in through the open doorway. Beyond the foyer was a sunken living area with a fireplace filling one wall. She took a timid step forward. Along the back were tall windows, revealing a circular brick patio and manicured yard. Her breath caught. It was perfect. If she'd been picking out a house this would have been the one she chose.

The corner of her mouth lifted a little. The living area's massive space held only a leather sofa, matching chair and large TV. How like a man to have only the essentials. What would it be like to snuggle up on that sofa next to Gabe in front of the fire? Something she wouldn't be doing. "You have a beautiful home."

She watched his lips curve up. Was he pleased with her compliment? Did it matter to him what she thought?

"Come on in and I'll show you around."

He led her through the living area, giving her time to admire the backyard anew through the windows as she followed him into the kitchen by way of a bay-window alcove that served as an eating area. A small table and two well-worn chairs were stationed there. The kitchen was spacious, furnished with all the latest appliances. She could only imagine what a pleasure it would be to cook for a family here. Hardly the galley-sized kitchen she'd been using.

It was a shame that no woman would share this house with him. If it was her… No, those thoughts were better left alone. That was one place she didn't need to go. He'd already made it clear what he wanted out of life and that didn't include her.

From there he pointed down a small hallway. "That's my suite and the way out to the carport. This is the way to your side of the house."

It might be, but she was afraid it wouldn't be far enough. Just being near him had her dreaming of what could be.

They crossed the living area and went through an arched doorway into a hallway that ran from the front of the house to the back.

"You have a choice between two bedrooms. You can have them both if you want them." Gabe turned to the right, bumping her as he did so. He grabbed her before she rocked backward. "Whoa there. We wouldn't want you to fall."

Gabe's hands were brand hot on her waist. He watched

her intently for a moment. His eyes focused on her lips before he released a breath he'd apparently been holding and let her go.

Zoe tingled all over with the desire to have him touch her again. Living in such a virile man's home wouldn't be easy.

He led her into a sunny room at the front of the house. It was larger than she'd had in her apartment. The street was out the front window and a neighbor's house could be seen in the distance through the other. "There's a full bath right there." Gabe pointed to a doorway. "The other room's down this way."

He didn't give her time to look before he walked out into the hallway. He acted as if he was making a point to keep as much distance as he could from her. Zoe caught up with him by the time he reached the doorway of the other room. This one was as large as the first but the view was nicer. From the window facing the back she could see the yard and trees.

"There's another bath in here." Gabe stood in the entrance and flipped on a light switch. "This bath isn't quite as large as the other one but it's a nice size."

He sounded almost apologetic. Did it really matter to him what she thought of it?

As she pondered those unsettling questions, he added, "You're welcome to store anything you like in the room you don't use."

"I appreciate that, but I've already put stuff in storage. I'll just be bringing my bedroom suite, a chair and TV. That should be enough. The less I bring, the less I have to worry about moving the second time." It was important she be practical about the arrangements because she *was not* living here long.

She caught sight of Gabe's odd expression a second

before he glanced away. "Whichever one you don't take I'll make the baby's room."

Her look met his again. "The baby will be living with me."

"I know that, but he or she will be regularly visiting me. I'll need a bedroom for my child."

His assertion solidified her resolve that when she was settled they were going to sit down and decide on Gabe's visitation schedule. His insistence on being involved wasn't going to overrule what she thought best for her baby. This was *her* baby. She would be making the final decisions about raising her child, regardless of what Gabe wanted. However, she knew this wasn't the time to broach that issue. She was juggling far too many things as it was. "We'll talk about your visitation rights later."

"Just because you keep putting it off, it doesn't mean the issue will go away. Or me, for that matter." He arched an eyebrow in challenge.

Before her temper got the better of her, Zoe headed for the front door. "I've got to get going. It's been a long day."

"Have you eaten? I could call for Chinese takeout or pizza."

She didn't slow down. "I have to go. I'll just do drive-through and go to bed early."

"Do you need any help moving? I can meet you Sunday morning."

Why did he keep being so nice to her? "Uh... No, I have it all taken care of. You've got your own stuff here to worry about." She walked out the front door but stopped on the porch. "By the way, did you have a chance to look at Mr. Luther's file?"

"I did. I plan to talk to his primary doctor just as soon as I can."

She stepped to him and touched his arm briefly.

That was a mistake. Even that had her blood humming. "Thanks, Gabe. I really appreciate it."

He glanced down before his earnest look met hers. "No problem, but still no promises."

"I understand." She smiled and removed her hand. "I'm grateful for any help you can offer him. See you on Sunday." She closed the door behind her and headed for her car.

As she slid into the driver's seat, Gabe stepped out onto the porch, his face unreadable. As she drove away, Zoe looked in her rearview mirror. Gabe was still standing there, hands in his pockets.

Why was she already missing him? He truly was a decent guy. She couldn't think of another person who would have been as understanding or helpful as he had been under the circumstances. Still, she must not forget he was only being so generous because of the baby. What would it be like to have someone like Gabe to come home to at the end of a weary day?

At least for a short while she and the baby had a nice place to live and, better yet, her mother was in a safe place that provided quality care. That was what really mattered.

Not the feelings Gabe brought out in her.

CHAPTER FOUR

LATE SUNDAY AFTERNOON, Zoe led the way in her compact car to Gabe's house. A couple of guys from work, John and Rick, were helping her move. They had managed to stay right behind her despite their trucks being heavy with her furniture and boxes of possessions.

She was grateful that Shorecliffs House encouraged residents to bring their own furniture when they moved in. Having familiar belongings around had definitely made her mother less anxious. To Zoe's surprise, her mother seemed content with her new residence.

In a few months Zoe would be living in her own place as well. If she could find the right small house she would buy. A child needed space, other families around them. A neighborhood similar to Gabe's.

She had managed to salvage the end tables in her living room. With those and one comfortable chair she'd bought with some of the insurance money, she planned to set up a small living area in her bedroom. That way she wouldn't disturb Gabe when he was home. If she didn't take steps to keep her distance, she could easily become too involved in his life. That wasn't what he wanted and she would respect that.

As Zoe pulled into the drive, Gabe stepped out onto the front porch. Had he been watching for her? She pulled as far up the driveway as she could so the two trucks would be as close as possible to the front door. Moments later she climbed out of the car and started toward him.

He wore a T-shirt and worn jeans with tennis shoes. His casual dress somehow made him even more attractive. It would be nice to have him greeting her when she came home every day. What was wrong with her? That fantasy she shouldn't entertain.

She joined John and Rick, who were already in the process of untying ropes securing her furniture. Gabe came down the two steps toward them.

"Gabe, this is John and Rick." She pointed to one then the other. "They work with me."

He shook hands with the men. "I'll get this end," he said to John as he pulled her headboard off the truck. Gabe maneuvered the bulky item, and then he led the way into the house with John carrying the other end.

Zoe pulled a box off and carried it inside. Gabe was on his way out of her room when she entered.

"You don't need to be carrying that. Give it here." His hands covered hers as he tried to take the box.

Awareness zipped through her. It was always there between them. Even the simplest touch from Gabe had her thinking of that night they had spent together. "I'm fine. It's not that heavy." She gave it a tug, removing his hands. "These guys can't spend all evening here. I need to help."

"Then why don't you just tell us where to put things and let us handle the moving?" Gabe followed her back to the room.

John glanced at them then slipped out the door.

She set the box down. "You need to understand right now that you do not tell me what I should or shouldn't do."

"And you need to think less about proving your independence and more about what's good for the baby. Now let us handle it."

Anger washed through Zoe as he left before she could

respond. A minute later Rick and John entered with the footboard. Gabe was right behind them with the rails. Gabe and John put the bed together while Rick returned to the truck. She pointed to the wall she wanted the bed against. Rick returned with a couple of boxes stacked on top of each other. All the men left once again. Zoe started removing bedsheets, pillows and a blanket from a box. She'd stay put and start unpacking if it would keep Gabe from making a scene.

All three men made a couple more trips to the truck.

After one trip she and Rick were left alone. He asked, nodding toward the doorway, "Who is this guy you're renting from?"

Before she could respond, Gabe entered the room with an end table and said in a tight tone, "I'm the father of her baby."

John came in right behind him. He and Rick looked at her with wonder then back at Gabe.

Holding up a hand, John said, "No offense, man. We just wanted to make sure Zoe was safe."

"None taken." Gabe's voice still held a hard note. "I'm sure she appreciates having friends who care about her." Gabe set the table down and stepped beside her.

"Come on, Rick." John tapped him on the shoulder. "We only have a couple more boxes."

"Why didn't you tell them who I am? Are you ashamed?" Gabe asked.

Zoe couldn't have been more shocked. Why would he believe that? He was an excellent doctor, well respected in his field, smart, had good taste in homes and, most of all, was a wonderful lover. Where had he gotten the idea she might be embarrassed by him? She couldn't imagine any woman not being proud of being associated with him. "I can assure you that's not the case. I just don't broadcast my private life. John and Rick are my friends but not that close."

"They sure sounded protective of you. I thought there might be more going on." His tone implied he might be jealous.

No man she knew even came close to measuring up to Gabe. She turned her head and gave him a questioning look. He had to care on some level to have those feelings, didn't he? Warmth flowed through her at the possibility. The self-assured man for once needed her reassurance. She stepped toward him. "Gabe, there's nothing to—"

"Well, that's it," Rick announced as he and John came in with a box apiece.

Zoe stepped away from Gabe but she felt his attention on her as he said, "Thanks, guys."

John and Rick headed for the front door, and she and Gabe followed.

There Gabe shook their hands, saying, "Thanks for your help. I appreciate it. I know Zoe does too."

There he was again, speaking for her. It made them sound like a couple. They weren't. "I do. I don't know what I'd have done without you guys." She hugged John then Rick. "I owe you big-time."

"Maybe you can make it up to us by bringing us some of your peanut-butter cookies. They're the best in the whole DC area."

Zoe was both flattered and embarrassed by such high praise of her cookies. She promised them a batch as soon as she settled in. They said their goodbyes.

"Thanks again," Zoe called and waved. She turned to see Gabe standing in the front doorway, leaning against the frame. Her nerves buzzed. Not only was she alone with him, she was now living in his house. She walked toward him. "Well, I guess I'll go finish straightening my room."

"Wouldn't you like to sit down for a few minutes? Have

something to eat. Not that I have anything here. I was going to order a pizza."

"I should get some unpacking done. I have to be at work early in the morning. I've been gone for a week." For some reason she needed to get to her room, take a moment for herself without Gabe nearby.

Gabe followed her more slowly into the house. Had he made the right decision by inviting Zoe to live at his house? Could he have offered a different solution to her living arrangements? He'd never counted on this attraction roaring through him. He had to keep his emotions in check. Focus on the baby and not the mother. It would be tough, but he would manage it.

Zoe was hiding from him. He was as certain of that fact as he was his name. She wasn't the type to run from problems. She had more than shown her ability to handle difficult circumstances. Yet he didn't doubt his judgment. He'd give her space. He still had boxes of his own to empty.

While he worked in the kitchen, he listened for sounds from the other side of the house. There were none. It was as if Zoe wasn't even there. Unable to stand it any longer, he walked softly to her room. As he was about to knock on the open door, he saw her. She lay sound asleep curled up in a ball on the half-made bed. After the last few days she'd had, or the week, she must be exhausted. He spied a blanket on the cushioned chair near the rear window. Picking it up, he placed it over her.

Zoe moaned and pulled the edge of the blanket up under her chin.

She looked so peaceful. Beautiful, with her eyelashes resting against her creamy skin. This was the woman who was the mother of his child. Would she look like Zoe? *She.* Did he want a daughter? Could he be a good father to a daughter? Girls needed special care. He wasn't even sure he could give what was needed to a son.

Zoe would make an excellent mom. He had no doubt of that. The care and concern she'd given the boy at the airport when he was hurt and the love she'd shown her mother all indicated he was right. As open and expressive as she had been with her friends when she'd thanked them for helping her was just another sign of her capacity to love. He could take lessons from her.

He'd been jealous of John and Rick when they had arrived. Had been resentful of the carefree way she'd treated them, especially when she seemed so guarded around him. He would like him and Zoe to at least be close friends. They had been friends at least during that one fateful night. Surely they could build on that beginning? Their baby at least deserved that kind of parental unity.

Unfortunately, standing here and staring down at Zoe wouldn't win him any friendship points if she woke. Unable to stop himself, he ran the back of a finger along her cheek. Zoe sighed. She truly was lovely. Before he got into trouble, he slowly lowered his hand and backed out of the room.

A couple of hours later he was waiting for his pizza to arrive when a loud "Dang it," followed by a crash, came from the direction of Zoe's room. Gabe ran across the house and down the hall as fast as the twists and turns would allow. When he reached the doorway, his heart almost stopped. Zoe teetered as she stood on the cushioned chair with a hammer in her hand. Around her on the carpet was a broken frame and pieces of glass. She rocked back. Gabe rushed forward, catching her against his chest.

The feel of her in his arms brought back erotic memories: hot kisses, tender caresses and willing woman opening in welcome... Desire like he'd never felt before washed over him. He must master his libido or he'd scare her.

As he lowered her to the floor, his protective instinct

propelled his hands to her waist to steady her. The curve there was no longer tiny, but knowing the reason for the change excited him all over again. Without thought, his hands moved to her middle. The gentle bulge fascinated him. *His child.* He'd never planned to have one, but now he was and everything about the miracle filled him with awe.

Zoe leaned back against him for a second then straightened.

The part of him better left dormant reacted once more to her nearness. His lips brushed her temple.

She stiffened and stepped away. "I'd better clean this mess up."

"I have a pizza coming. You're welcome to some." He moved to the door. "Don't stand on anything again. Call me if you need to do something above your head."

Zoe went down on her knees and started picking up broken pieces. She still hadn't looked at him. "Okay."

Her tone implied she wasn't promising anything.

"Zoe." He waited until she looked up and into his eyes. "I mean it."

Her expression went hard. "I heard you. But I thought I made it clear to you earlier you have no right to tell me what to do while I'm here."

He wasn't going to allow her to push away the importance of what had almost happened just now. "Then I suggest you think through what you're about to do before you act on it. You or the baby or both could have been seriously hurt if I hadn't been here to catch you."

"Ow!" She stared at her hand.

He took an involuntary step toward her. "What happened?"

"I cut my hand." A stream of blood ran over her palm.

"Give me that." Gabe took the pieces of glass from her and dumped them into a trash can nearby. Cupping her elbow, he helped her stand. Reaching over his shoulder, he grabbed a handful of his shirt and pulled.

"What're you doing?" Zoe asked, the pitch of her voice rising in alarm.

"Taking off my shirt to use as a bandage," Gabe explained impatiently, his words muffled by the material covering his head.

"Isn't that a little dramatic?"

Pulling the shirt off, he retorted, "Not if you don't want blood on the new carpet or one of your towels." He glanced around. "Even if we could find one." He wrapped the shirt around her hand and applied pressure. "I have a first-aid kit in the kitchen. Go into the bathroom and clean up. I'll be right back."

Gabe returned to find Zoe had obeyed his instruction, which surprised him. He had fully expected her to argue or defy him. Putting the kit on the counter, he opened it. After a quick search he found a bandage and removed the covering. "Let me have a look. I want to make sure you don't have any glass in the wound."

"I cleaned it well. There's nothing there. Hand me the bandage and I'll put it on."

Gabe ignored her, seizing her hand and turning it palm up. The bleeding had stopped but there was a fine line of red across the pad, gaping slightly at the center. He looked closely for any slivers. "Does it hurt anywhere?"

"No." Her breath brushed his bare shoulder, setting his pulse humming.

They were so close. Her sweet scent filled his head. He reached for the bandage and applied one end of it. "Hold this end."

She placed her finger where he indicated, and he pulled off the paper cover of the other adhesive strip, smoothing the bandage into place. Her hand felt so fragile, soft. He ran his fingertip along the line in the center of her palm. Zoe shivered.

Her gaze met his. Time hung suspended. Their faces were so close. His attention fell on her full lips. He'd wanted to taste them earlier but had stopped himself. Here was his chance again. All he had to do was lean forward the least bit to experience them. Did he dare? Would she let him?

Want like a live sizzling wire buzzed through him. His gaze met Zoe's again. She was watching him, eyes wide with questions. Did she need his kisses as much as he wanted to give them? His mouth moved toward hers as if it had a mind of its own.

The tip of Zoe's tongue darted out to dampen her bottom lip before her eyes fluttered closed. His blood heated and his body jerked to attention. Her actions were the confirmation he'd been waiting for. There was no stopping him now. A second later his mouth found hers.

The touch of Zoe's lips was all he remembered and more. So much more. Her mouth, plump and inviting, pulled him in. This wasn't the flurry and fiery urgency of that one torrid night. Instead it was slow, easy, experimental, answering questions and creating so many more.

Zoe sighed softly and leaned into him, her hands running up his chest. His arms circled her waist, bringing her against him. Gabe deepened the kiss. Zoe opened for him, eagerly greeted him. Her fingers played with the hair at the nape of his neck as his hands roamed her back, before pulling her tighter. She tasted so good.

The doorbell rang.

Zoe jerked away. Her eyes were wild like a startled animal looking to escape. "We shouldn't have done that."

Gabe leaned to kiss her again. He hadn't had enough. "We've done far more."

Her hands fanned across his chest, pushing, stopping

him. "Gabe, we don't want the same things. You don't want a spouse or the full-time responsibility of a family. I do. We aren't living together. I'm your roommate. I only moved in here because I couldn't think of what else to do. If you cannot respect my boundaries, I'll have to find another place to go."

Anger flared in him. It was obvious she felt the attraction he did. The spontaneous spark of their kiss was undeniable proof. Yet she was steeling herself, refusing to act on it. His eyes met Zoe's, held. "Don't go. I'll keep my hands to myself. I'll stay in my half of the house."

The bell rang again.

"I'd better get that before the delivery guy leaves." At the door he stopped and turned back to her. "Just know this. You'll have to do the asking next time."

Zoe stood in the bathroom, shaking. Her heated blood zipped through her trembling body. She looked into the mirror. A woman who had been thoroughly kissed stared back at her. Bright eyes, rose-tinted cheeks and swollen lips all told the story. Zoe ran her fingers over her still tingling mouth.

Every fiber of her body wanted to rush to Gabe and tell him she wanted him to touch her again. Kiss her. Love her. Yet her coldly rational mind said no. There would be nothing but pain if she once more allowed her body to overrule her heart. She couldn't let her desire for him control what she really wanted.

Gabe hadn't even suggested marriage as a convenient means of helping her with the responsibilities and mounting expenses of being pregnant by him. Oh, he was being noble, very nice, and even willing to "pay his share" of the expenses of her pregnancy, but nothing more. From what she'd learned about Gabe, he would have done the same for any other woman he'd accidentally impregnated.

Even if he had asked, she wouldn't have accepted. What if he left her when he felt his obligation was over? She wouldn't survive. Nothing but a commitment born of love was enough for her.

Her breath had caught when he'd pulled off his shirt. She'd seen him shirtless before but the light had been dim. This time she could make out every nuance of his wide, muscular shoulders. She'd not missed the flex of his arm muscles as he'd applied the bandage or the light dusting of hair in the center of his chest narrowing into a line leading beneath the waist of his jeans. Large enough to carry heavy loads, both physically and metaphorically, it would be so easy to let him share her burdens without that all-important commitment of love.

Gabe smelled of male heat and his own special musk. His scent surrounded her. She was tempted to inhale deeply, memorize it, only to realize she already had. His tender touch had undone her as his finger had traveled over her palm. She wanted more of his kisses. Longed for his lips to cover hers again. All her vows to herself had evaporated like water on a hot day the second his mouth had found hers. There had been no thinking, only feeling. Only Gabe for that one eternal moment.

Thankfully the pizza guy had arrived, snapping her back to reality.

"Food's in the kitchen if you want any," Gabe called.

She was hungry and had to face him sometime. Also, she'd made her reasons for rejecting him crystal clear. There was no purpose in avoiding him with the ground rules of their relationship established. The aroma of cheese and tomato sauce drew her to the kitchen.

Gabe had pulled on another shirt and now sat at the table with the pizza box open and a slice in his hand. A canned drink sat in front of him.

"I haven't had time to go to the grocery. Help yourself

to a soda. If you'd rather have water, the glasses are to the right of the sink."

Apparently, Gabe had recovered from their moment in the bathroom. He was treating her like the roommate she'd asked him to. So why wasn't she more pleased about it? "Thanks."

Gabe didn't even look her direction while she filled her glass with water and took her chair. He pushed the box toward her. She selected a slice. "We haven't talked about any house rules."

He gave her an incredulous look. "There are no house rules. You're free to do as you please. Treat it as yours. There don't have to be rules for everything."

His aggravation rang clear in his tone. Had she pushed him too far? Her common sense kicked in. All she'd done was hold to her vow, hold her ground about what their relationship would be while she lived here. His ego was no doubt bruised, but what was he really after? The best she could tell was sex while he waited for his child to be born.

"Thanks. It would be nice to use the kitchen. I like to cook healthily, especially for the baby."

"Then cook to your heart's content." He took another bite of his pizza. After swallowing, he asked, "Do you mind if I ask you a question?"

What was he after now? Was he going to put her on the spot about what had happened a few minutes ago? Her feelings about him? "No. Ask away."

"Why did you pick the room you did?"

That particular question was totally unexpected. Why would he care? "Because of the view. I like the trees and the yard."

He nodded thoughtfully.

Gabe had her curiosity up now. "Why do you want to know?"

"I just wondered if you saw the front room as a nursery and chose the other for that reason." He watched her.

"Truthfully, I didn't, but it would make a lovely one with all the natural light."

"Then that's what I'll make it. I need to do something with this place. I was thinking of hiring an interior decorator to help. Unless you would like to do the room. After all, you'll be here for a little while after the baby is born."

"I'll think about it." Could she stand to see her dream nursery become reality and then leave it? Yet the thought of bringing the baby home to a pretty little world excited her.

Gabe didn't offer any more conversation. And she couldn't find a comfortable way to initiate one. She didn't like this stilted silence between them. He must be angrier about her rejection than she'd first thought.

"Do you want another slice?" he finally asked.

She shook her head.

Closing the box, he stood. "Well, I'm going to call it a night. I need to be at the hospital early on my first day." He walked to the refrigerator, opened it and put the box inside. "I'll see what I can do about Mr. Luther as soon as I can. It may not be tomorrow. Night." With that he went down the hall toward his room.

Zoe sat looking out at the dark patio, feeling deflated. Something was missing. Something she hadn't known was special until it had gone. Zoe glanced in the direction Gabe had gone. She wanted it back.

"Hey, I forgot to give you this."

Zoe jumped at Gabe's voice. She hadn't heard him returning. He was barefooted and bare-chested with only a pair of sports shorts riding his slim hips.

He slid a key across the table toward her. "You'll need that."

"Uh…thanks."

"I'll see about getting you a garage door opener as soon as possible so you can park in the carport."

"Okay."

"Night, Zoe."

"Good night." She watched him leave, wishing she was going with him.

After putting her glass in the dishwasher, she straightened the kitchen and put the chairs back into place before going to her room. Stepping into her bathroom brought back memories of Gabe's kiss. Would it be like that every time she went in? She feared it would.

Moving in with Gabe had been a calculated risk. One she'd believed she could handle, but it was proving more difficult than she had anticipated. Yet her mother now had the quality care she needed, deserved, so the risk Zoe was taking with her heart was worth it. At least living with Gabe was temporary. Knowing there was a time limit on the intense temptation did help.

Tonight was an example of why she needed to strengthen her resolve to keep their relationship on a business basis. There would be no more moments of weakness on her part if she could prevent it.

After a hot bath she crawled under the covers. She'd never felt more alone in her life. Gabe was only steps away, but she wouldn't go to him. What would it be like to sleep with her head on his shoulder? Heaven. Yet she couldn't allow herself even the pleasure of that fantasy because it would weaken her self-control.

CHAPTER FIVE

GABE HAD FORGOTTEN what it was like to start a new job. The stress, anxiety and the feeling of always being one step behind. He didn't like that. Knowing what was happening in his sphere of influence was important to him. Indirectly Zoe had accused him of being controlling. In her case and with his patients, he believed it was more about caring. Either way, he was determined he would be placed on the surgery schedule sooner rather than later. The more surgery he did, the faster his career would grow.

Even in the OR there was an adjustment period. It would take time to put a staff together that would interact smoothly with each other. For now it would be trial and error. Yet this was the position he'd been working toward his entire professional life. What he hadn't planned for was becoming a father while trying to create the finest liver-transplant program in the world.

Worse was his growing desire for his "roommate."

It had been three days since he'd seen Zoe and he didn't anticipate slowing down long enough to see her anytime soon. If she'd been worried they'd have too much time together, these past few days had proved her concern groundless. As far as he could tell, she was asleep when he came home and getting her morning shower when he left. He'd known his job would be demanding and had accepted it. That was just one of a number of reasons why he wouldn't make a long-term commitment to a woman.

Since he'd not seen Zoe after giving her a house key, he'd left his garage door opener on the kitchen counter because he had not had time to get another. He wrote her a note.

This is for you. Sorry I didn't think to give it to you the other night. Been busy. Call me if you need something.

When he pulled into the drive late that night, Zoe's car wasn't parked in her usual spot, just to the right past the front door. A light burned in the kitchen. She must have taken him up on his offer to park in the carport now she had a door opener.

He studied the glow in the window. At least Zoe had thought about him. He'd been living with his mother the last time he'd come home to a light left on for him. There was something about it that said, *I care about you.*

As he entered the front door, a wonderful smell filled the air. Making his way to the kitchen, he discovered a plate of cookies with a note beside them. He dropped his keys and picked up the piece of paper.

Made some for the guys. Thought you might like a few.

Gabe took a bite of a peanut-butter cookie. "Mmm." His grandmother used to bake them. His mother never had much time for that sort of thing. Most of her efforts revolved around her job. Her actions had taught him that success was only gained through hard work and personal sacrifice. Picking up the plate, he flipped off the light and headed for his bedroom with a smile. He would eat the rest before he went to bed.

The next morning he left another note.

Thanks for the cookies. They hit the spot.

Note-passing wasn't as satisfying as seeing Zoe, but at least they weren't ignoring each other.

How good her cookies were was on his mind as he started his rounds just after noon. The first patient he planned to see was Mr. Luther. Gabe had contacted Mr. Luther's physician, Dr. Patel, and they had agreed that he should be transferred to Gabe's care. Mr. Luther's health had deteriorated to the point where a transplant was the only option. The hepatitis C had taken its toll. Following Dr. Patel's instructions, Mr. Luther was admitted to National Hospital for an evaluation before being placed on the liver transplant list.

Gabe rapped his knuckles on the door.

A gruff voice called, "Come in."

Gabe pushed the door open. "Mr. Luther, I'm..." He stopped short. Zoe stood at the bedside of a grizzly man who obviously hadn't shaved in a number of days.

"Gab—uh... Dr. Marks, hello." Zoe's smile was cautious.

His heart gave a little extra beat. "I hadn't expected to see you."

"I wasn't sure if I'd see you either." She looked at him shyly.

"Thanks for the cookies. They were great."

She glanced toward their patient, who was looking from one of them to the other with curiosity, and said to Gabe, "It's part of my job to keep tabs on Mr. Luther."

The older man pointed first at Gabe then at her and

back again. "I'm guessing you two know each other, him eating your cookies and all."

Gabe nodded, stepping forward and extending his hand. "I'm Dr. Marks. Dr. Patel has thoroughly reviewed your case with me."

"So you're why I'm in one of these dang uncomfortable beds again." He didn't sound happy but shook Gabe's hand.

Zoe placed her hand on the man's other arm. "Mr. Luther, Dr. Marks is going to help you. If you want to blame someone, it should be me. I asked him to see you."

Gabe couldn't believe how big a heart Zoe had. She was emotionally invested in her patient far more than was required by her job. Was Mr. Luther an exception to her rule or did she, as Gabe suspected, care deeply about all her patients, and Mr. Luther in particular? What would it be like to be under her umbrella of loving concern? *Focus on your patient*, Gabe sternly ordered himself. "She did ask me, and the first thing I need to do is examine you. Then we'll run some tests."

"More of them, you mean," the man grunted.

Gabe shrugged and removed his stethoscope from around his neck. "Now, would you lean forward for me?"

The man did as he asked and Gabe listened to his heart. He then had him breathe deeply as he checked out his lungs. "I'm going to turn this overhead light on. I need to look at your eyes."

The switch was on Zoe's side of the bed and she flipped it on.

"I've not spoken to his nurse yet, so I don't know his vitals, Zoe. Would you mind getting his BP for me? Check his pulse points?" Gabe placed his stethoscope around his neck and removed a penlight from his pocket.

She laid the folder in her hand on a chair and went to work.

Gabe looked at the man. "I understand you were diagnosed with hepatitis a number of years ago."

"Yeah." Mr. Luther nodded.

"When did you first seek help for it?" Gabe looked into his eyes.

"Maybe six months ago."

"He was referred to the Liver Alliance by Dr. Patel three months ago," Zoe said, as she placed the cuff on the patient's arm. She pumped the cuff then listened through her stethoscope for his pulse. Done, she looked at him. "One-thirty over ninety."

Gabe nodded. "Not perfect but not as bad as I expected. Mr. Luther, have you been a heavy drinker in the past?"

The man glared at him. "I've drunk."

Gabe gave him a pointed look in return. "You do understand that there can be no drinking again if you have a transplant."

"I'm not even sure I want a transplant," the man grumbled.

Zoe looked up from where she was checking Mr. Luther's pulses on his feet. "Mr. Luther, you need to think hard about that. Without it you'll die."

"Gonna die one day anyway."

Gabe slipped his penlight back into his pocket. "That's true, but without a new liver you have at best a couple of years and you'll get increasingly sicker. There won't be much quality to your life. We're going to do the workup on you to consider listing you for a transplant, but you need to know that your attitude will affect the decision-making. New livers are hard to come by. If you're not going to do your part to keep a new liver healthy, you'll not be listed."

"Yeah." The man picked up the TV remote. "I'll think about it." He nodded toward Zoe. "I'd better not hear that you've been giving Avery here a hard time or you'll answer to me."

"Noted." Gabe made eye contact with Zoe and nodded toward the door. She gave the man a concerned look and followed him out.

Zoe closed the door behind her and looked at him with such hope. "So what do you think?"

Gabe shook his head slightly. "I'm really concerned about his compliance. He's a gruff bear, I know, but to be listed, the committee must know he'll do what he's supposed to do."

"I'll talk to him. Make it clear."

"*He* has to want this," Gabe stated emphatically. "You have done all you can do for him by bringing him to my attention."

Zoe glared at him. "I know that."

"Even if he does agree to cooperate, I can't guarantee he'll be a candidate. I'm just one person on a committee of eight."

She touched his arm. "I appreciate you trying."

Gabe nodded. He hated that he couldn't give her more encouragement. "I have to go. I have other patients to visit."

That evening, Gabe found a note from Zoe waiting on the counter.

There's supper in the refrigerator if you're interested. Thanks for all you're doing for Mr. Luther.

He felt himself smiling, unable to contain his satisfaction. Why was this particular patient so important to her? Even though he'd not given Zoe much reassurance on Mr. Luther's prognosis, she was expressing her gratitude by cooking for him.

He'd not eaten since lunch, so he was tickled to have a home-cooked meal. His day had been so exhausting he'd not even bothered to get drive-through. Zoe's cooking, even though it would be rewarmed, was heaven sent. He could get used to this treatment.

Gabe had just sat down at the table when the patter of feet drew his attention. Looking over his shoulder, he saw Zoe. He smiled, glad to see her. Her appearance, on top of her meal, was totally unexpected.

She wore a short fleece robe tied above the rise of her belly. His gut clenched with pride. That bump was his child. Had he ever seen a more beautiful sight? Zoe's hair was mussed as if she had been running her fingers through it in angst. Was she nervous about approaching him? Why should she be? She'd recovered her self-control the moment the doorbell had interrupted their bathroom interlude.

"Hey," Gabe said. "Thanks for the meal."

"You're welcome."

"Sorry if I woke you." He picked up his fork, ready to take a bite.

Zoe said softly, "I've been waiting up for you."

She had? Hope, warm as a fire, welled in his chest. "Really?"

"I wanted to talk to you about my rent."

Disappointment smothered his anticipation. She wanted to talk about that now? Shaking his head in refusal, he turned back to the food. "I've had a long day. Make that a week. I'm in no mood to talk business now."

Zoe moved around the table, facing him. "I have to pay for my mother's housing, so I need to know what my budget will be."

That made perfect sense, but it didn't give him the energy to hash out her rent right this minute. "Then make it a dollar for this month. When I get time, I'll figure something out."

She leaned toward him slightly, giving him an amazing

view of cleavage. Her breasts were larger than he remembered. Pregnancy had changed her there as well.

She announced with more volume than necessary, "I'm not just paying you a dollar!"

With effort, he turned his attention to cutting his pork chop. "Then you decide what you can afford to pay when you work out your budget. Right now, I'm hungry and don't want to talk about it. Instead, why don't you sit down and keep me company? Tell me how your mother's doing."

He glanced up in time to catch her perplexed look as she slowly sank into the other chair.

She didn't immediately start talking, so between bites he asked, "So? How is she?"

"Still confused but otherwise okay. The staff assures me she's adjusting quite well."

A moment of silence followed, and then Zoe remarked, "You know, you really should take better care of yourself. You're eating like you haven't had anything all day."

He shrugged. "That's pretty close to the truth."

"Gabe!"

"Yeah?" He met her look as he poked his fork at some green beans.

"You've got to do better than that. You can't keep that up."

This was the tables being turned. He was the one who normally scolded her. Now her anxiety was for him. He liked it. "Thanks for your concern. I do appreciate it. But I have my hands full at work. I've had to hit the ground running every day since I started. Hopefully it'll get better soon." He cut into the pork chop again. Lifting the piece on the end of his fork, he said, "This sure is good."

"I'm glad you like it. You know if you don't start taking care of yourself you won't be healthy enough to care for your patients."

He finished off the last of the roasted potatoes, wishing there were more. She was a good cook. Or maybe the food was made better by the fact that someone had cared enough to think of him. It would be so easy to get used to, even if she'd done it out of gratitude. "Zoe, I know you look after the welfare of others all the time, but I can take care of myself. I'm all right."

"What makes you think you can give me a place to live for virtually nothing because you're concerned enough to help me, but I can't respond in kind?"

She had him there. It made him feel good having someone waiting for him at home who would talk to him over a freshly cooked meal, instead of always eating carryout or fast food in front of the TV. Yet Zoe had made it very clear that she was only renting space from him, that they were not "living together." It was time to move the conversation off him. "Give me until this weekend to think about the rent and I'll have a figure. Will that do?"

"I can wait that long. There's one more thing I wanted to talk to you about."

Gabe almost groaned out loud. He was in no mood for this. If he had to have a discussion with her, he'd rather discuss whether or not she preferred being kissed on the neck or behind the ear. "And that is?"

"I noticed you haven't bought any food. I'm planning to stop by the grocery on my way home tomorrow. Would you like me to pick up some things for you?"

"Uh… I usually eat at the hospital or get takeout." She frowned at that, so he amended, "But you've made an excellent point about taking better care of myself. I do need to have something here. If you don't mind, could you get a few boxes of mac and cheese, some frozen dinners and protein bars? That should hold me until I can get to the store myself. Take the cost out of your rent when we settle on the amount."

She turned up her lip and looked down her nose at him.

"That's your list? As a doctor, you should be ashamed of yourself."

He shrugged. "You asked."

"I did. Well, I'd better get to bed." She rose. "Night, Gabe."

He watched her walk away. The more distance she put between them, the cooler the room became. If only he was going with her. "Good night," he whispered when she was out of sight.

Gabe finished his dinner, put the dirty plate into the sink, flipped off the light and went to his lonely room. With any luck, he was so tired he would go to sleep quickly and not think about the desirable woman just steps away. Was this what his life would be like? Always wishing for more?

Two evenings later Gabe came home before it was dark for the first time in a week. He'd had a replacement garage door opener for the one he gave Zoe delivered to the hospital, so he was now able to park beside Zoe's car in the carport. There was something strangely intimate about their cars sharing the same close space. He shook off that thought. Zoe didn't want that. Had made it very clear. Still, that didn't mean he hadn't lain awake late into the night, thinking about her.

Entering the house, he inhaled the delicious aroma of lasagna. He must be doing something right in Zoe's eyes. As he took another deep sniff, his stomach growled. Following the scent, he fully anticipated finding Zoe standing in the kitchen. Disappointment washed over him. She wasn't there. He headed toward her side of the house but along the way his attention was diverted out the window to the patio. There she was, sitting in a cheap fold-up lounger. Her head was back, her face lifted to the late-afternoon sun. Was she asleep?

Her head turned. Had she sensed he was there? Their gazes met through the glass, held. Zoe reminded him of an old master's painting where the yellow light surrounded her feminine form as if she was a heavenly being. That was the thought of a lovesick man. Which he was not!

Zoe blinked and half lifted the hand lying over their baby and waved. Gabe smiled and headed in her direction. She was a temptation he should stay away from but was drawn to as if he were in her gravity field. Stepping out of the French doors of the living room, he strolled across the patio.

"I'm surprised to see you home so early." Zoe looked back over her shoulder at him.

"I decided it was time to come home at a decent hour." He continued moving until he was facing her then nodded his head toward the house. "Something smells delicious. Do you have enough for two?" Did he sound as pitiful as he felt?

She smiled. "Yes. I made enough so that I'd have some to leave in the refrigerator for you."

Even after their somewhat strained conversation a couple of nights ago, she was still trying to take care of him. Doing it despite her insistence that they were nothing more than roommates. He suppressed a spark of hope she'd changed her mind and managed to answer in a neutral tone, "Thanks. That's really nice of you."

"It's the least I can do since you're helping me out."

That explanation left a sour taste in his mouth. He would've liked it better if her kindness was motivated by a more intimate reason. Why did he keep wishing for more? She'd made it so plain on numerous occasions there would be nothing between them but the baby. He needed to accept it and get on with his personal life. Maybe it was time to ask about the available female staff at the hospital.

Zoe was saying, "I'd better get up and take it out before it burns. If you hadn't come home it really might have. The sun feels so good." Zoe swung her feet off the lounger to the bricks. "The day is so beautiful I couldn't pass up the chance to be outside. I saw this lounger in the grocery and had to have it."

Gabe stepped closer. "I'm sorry there's no patio furniture. I've never had a need for it before."

"This is such a nice space I'd furnish it before anything else." A shocked look came over her face. "I'm sorry. That's none of my business."

"Why can't it be? As far as I'm concerned, you can have a say in how I furnish the house where our child will be spending a lot of time. I don't know anything about that stuff. How about going with me to pick something out? You'd have a better idea of what I need than I do." He wasn't sure what had made him extend the invitation, but any reason that might coax her into spending time with him was worth a try.

She looked at him as if weighing the pros and cons. "I guess I could, if you really want me to."

"Tomorrow work for you?" The question had just popped out. He'd had no intention of doing it that soon.

"I have to visit Mother first thing in the morning, but I could go after that."

"Great! We'll go visit your mom then head for the furniture store. I've not seen where she's living, and I'd like to."

"Why?" She watched him suspiciously.

"Why what?"

Her look didn't waver. "Why would you want to go with me to visit my mother?"

He couldn't really answer that, so he settled on, "Because I like your mother and she'll be the grandmother of my child. Also, you've practically gone into debt because of the quality of this place, so I'm curious."

Zoe shrugged then pushed off the lounger. When she teetered backward, he caught her elbow and helped her stand. Her chuckle was a nervous one. "Thanks. I'm getting more off balance by the day. If you want to go, you can. I need to get the lasagna out." She walked toward the door.

Gabe followed her. *And more beautiful.* In the kitchen, he watched while Zoe removed and cut the pasta. He could hardly wait to taste it. To resist digging in before it made it to a plate, he busied himself with the dishes.

"I'm impressed. A man who knows how to set the table correctly." Zoe picked up a plate and returned to the stove.

"My grandmother taught me. She'd be happy you noticed." He took glasses from the shelf and filled them with ice.

"Not your mother?"

"Mom wasn't around much. She was busy making a living. I spent a good deal of time with my grandmother in my early years." Why was he telling her all of this? He didn't make a habit of sharing his personal life.

"You must've missed your mom."

He had. She'd told him throughout his childhood that it must be that way since his father was gone. Gabe's child was never going to know that feeling if he could help it. But would that really be possible with his current job, the future demands of his career? "I did, but it was what it was."

Zoe looked at him for a moment as if she understood everything he wasn't saying. Moving to the table, she set down the plate of food. "Go ahead and start. It's better hot." Picking up the other plate, she returned to the stove.

Gabe finished pouring the tea and took his place. Zoe had included a small salad and a piece of toasted bread as well. The aroma was divine but still he waited for her.

Zoe joined him with her plate in her hand. "I told you to go ahead and start."

"And my grandmother taught me that the cook deserves to be waited for. Sorry, her teaching trumps what you want."

Zoe smiled. "Smart woman."

"She was. I miss her every day." Zoe reminded him of his grandmother, who had been the most giving and caring person he'd ever known until he'd met Zoe.

"Tell me about her." Zoe placed her napkin in her lap and picked up her fork.

"I guess she was like every other grandmother. Tough when she needed to be but loving all the time." Gabe took a bite of the hot lasagna and his taste buds screamed with joy. Zoe could get a permanent job cooking for him. He would miss her when she left. That looming event he didn't want to think about. "This is wonderful. I didn't think anything could be any better than the meal last night."

Her eyes twinkled and her cheeks turned rosy. She enjoyed a compliment. Had the other men in her life not done that enough? He'd like her to always look at him the way she was now. In spite of her curt refusal to allow a personal relationship between them, her happiness mattered very much to him. But why?

"I'm glad you like it," Zoe said with a hint of shyness. As if she hadn't been sure he would.

"Anyone would."

"Not anyone."

There it was. Just what he'd suspected. "Has someone said you weren't a good cook?"

Zoe made a sound low in her throat. "Oh, yeah, in no uncertain terms."

Annoyance hot as fire flashed through him on her behalf. "Like who?"

"My ex-fiancé. Nothing I prepared for him seemed to

suit. He always complained. Too salty, too hot. I guess that's one of the reasons he's my ex. Along with a few other, larger character flaws."

She'd been engaged? Had cared about a man enough to want to marry him? It shocked Gabe how much that bothered him. If she'd married that guy, they wouldn't be sitting here now. Wouldn't have had that night or be expecting a baby. He would have missed knowing Zoe. He swallowed hard and put his fork down. "What happened?"

"I caught him out to dinner with another woman. Turned out he was a jerk. He made it embarrassingly clear in front of the entire restaurant that I wasn't who he wanted. That I was too old-fashioned. Wasting my time waiting for a knight in silver armor to ride up and pledge to love me until death did us part. That expecting the man who said he loved me to be faithful and plan to be with me forever was naive nonsense. He said I needed to grow up. What a fool I was! I know what I want, and I have no intention of settling or compromising."

Gabe had the sudden urge to hit something. If her ex had been there he would have punched him in the face. Although he was pretty sure he wouldn't like the answer to the question before he asked it, he couldn't stop himself. "What do you want?"

"To find someone who will love me for who I am. Who'll put me first in his life and grow old with me." She looked at him. "To have that happily ever after."

Her answer was worse than he'd expected. She wanted everything Gabe was confident he couldn't provide.

CHAPTER SIX

ZOE WOKE THE next morning to the sun shining through her bedroom window and the birds chirping. She stretched. Now that she was well into her second trimester, she was feeling more energetic. A flutter in her middle made her pause. She couldn't stop a smile of happiness curving her lips. The baby was kicking. Butterfly taps, but they were there nonetheless.

At dinner after she'd told Gabe she was holding out for a man who would love her unconditionally and commit the rest of his life to their marriage and family, the conversation had become stilted, punctuated by awkward silence. His reaction had not been a surprise. It had merely reinforced his original revelation that he had no interest in getting married and having a family. With his logic, his career wouldn't allow it. When she'd risen to clean the kitchen, he'd insisted he would do it. Sensing Gabe was still uncomfortable with her answer, she'd left him to it and gone to bed. She'd slept well and deeply.

Thinking about the way their evening had ended, she feared their visit to her mother's and the shopping trip might be tense as well. Debating whether or not to spend the day with Gabe, she was surprised by the smell of frying bacon wafting into her room.

Gabe was cooking?

She pulled her robe on and tugged the belt tight, making certain she was completely covered. More than once when she'd been talking to Gabe about rent, she'd caught his gaze slipping to the V of her robe. His hot glances had brought to mind passionate memories that would have weakened her resolve if she'd allowed herself to revisit them.

The scent led her to the kitchen, where Gabe stood at the stove with his bare back to her, the view of wide shoulders with thick muscles tapering to a trim waist and slim hips clad in well-worn jeans hung low. She swallowed. He had such a nice behind, was a magnificent specimen of a male. Her fingers twitched with the temptation to touch him. Would he mind if she did? The question set off mental alarm bells. She must stop tormenting herself with fantasies of forbidden pleasures.

She stuffed her hands into the pockets of her robe and cleared her throat. "Good morning."

Gabe half turned. "Morning. I don't have your culinary talents but I can cook eggs and bacon. Interested?"

Zoe battled to master her physical reaction to him as she shrugged in what she hoped was a nonchalant manner. "Sure."

"Have a seat. I'm just getting ready to do the eggs. How do you like yours?"

Apparently, whatever had been bothering him last night was forgotten. She took what had become her place at the table. "Scrambled."

He smiled. "Scrambled it is."

She liked this cheerful, relaxed version of Gabe. This was the man she'd gotten to know in Chicago. The charmer. She suspected his charisma was at full force.

Gabe placed a plate with fluffy eggs, two slices of crisp bacon and buttered toast in front of her. It looked as delicious as it smelled. She gave him a genuine smile of gratitude. "Thanks."

He soon joined her with a plate twice as full as hers in his hand. Over the next few minutes they ate in a companionable silence. Zoe was glad their camaraderie had returned. Slowly chewing bacon and studying him as he ate, she decided she'd like it to always be that way between them. She watched as his gaze met hers. He raised a brow.

"Thank you. This is wonderful."

Gabe looked pleased. "You're welcome."

His phone that was always nearby buzzed. He picked it up. "Dr. Marks."

As he talked she continued to eat, paying little attention to the conversation. "I'll be in this afternoon to review the charts." Gabe ended the call.

"Problem?"

"I implemented a new protocol. It's not popular, so I'm getting some pushback. Do you have a certain time that you have to be at your mother's?"

"It's Saturday, so I can go whenever I wish."

"Then do you think you can be ready to leave in half an hour? I have to go in to the hospital later." He picked up his toast.

She pushed at her eggs. "Then why don't you just go pick out furniture while I go see Mom? Cut down on your stress."

"No, I've got time. I just need to check the charts after shift change this afternoon."

She was amazed at his dedication to detail. "You really oversee all the details."

"It's important that my program be cutting-edge."

She pursed her lips and nodded. "Or you're just a bit of a control freak."

He grinned. "And maybe a little bit of that as well."

* * *

An hour and a half later they were walking into Shore-cliffs House.

"This looks nice," Gabe said as he held the front door open for her.

"It is, but I still hate that Mom can't take care of herself anymore and, worse, that I can't do it either."

Gabe's arm came around her and pulled her into a quick hug before dropping away.

"You're doing the best you can for your mother. She knows you love her."

Zoe wished his hug had lasted longer as she held back tears. "I hope so."

They walked down the long hall and took the first right, stopping in front of a door on the left. Zoe knocked. Pushing it open with some trepidation about what she would find, she was pleasantly surprised. Her mother sat in a cushioned chair near the window. A book lay on her lap. Zoe's heart lifted. Her mother had always loved reading, but Zoe hadn't seen her pick up a book in months. Even if she wasn't reading, at least she'd thought to try. "Hi, Mom."

Her mother looked up. A smile came across her face. "Hey, sweetheart."

Relief washed over Zoe. Today her mother recognized her. The doctors had told Zoe there would be times when her mom would know her and then her memory would fade again.

"How're you?" Her mother was having a good day.

Zoe smiled and kissed her on the cheek. "I'm doing fine." She sank into a nearby straight chair.

Her mother looked to where Gabe stood. "You brought someone with you."

"Hello, Mrs. Avery. It's nice to see you again," Gabe said as he stepped forward.

Her mother gave him a blank look but soon the brightness of recognition filled her eyes. "I know you. You brought chicken."

"That's right." Gabe sat on the edge of the bed. "How do you like your new place? It's nice, and your daughter has done a lovely job of furnishing it."

"I want to go home," she said earnestly.

Zoe's chest tightened. She hated hearing those words. Gabe reached over and took her hand, giving it a gentle, reassuring squeeze. She appreciated the support. It was good of him to notice her distress. "I know, Mom, but right now this is the best place for you."

"Can I go home?"

"Mrs. Avery, do you dance?" Gabe asked.

That was an odd question. Zoe was thankful for his timely redirection of her mother's thoughts, but was perplexed by the new topic of conversation he'd chosen.

"Dance?" her mother asked in a tone Zoe hadn't heard in a long time.

"I noticed on the activity board on our way down the hall that there's a dance on Saturday night. I was wondering if you were going." Gabe leaned forward as if greatly interested in her answer.

Her mother actually blushed. Zoe couldn't help but smile.

"I don't know."

"I bet there are a number of men who would like to dance with you," Zoe said to further encourage her. "I also saw that they have game day, music and people coming in to sing."

Her mother gave her a bleak look. Zoe had lost her again. She forged forward. "We're on our way to buy some furniture."

"Furniture?" her mom said.

"Yes. For my patio," Gabe answered.

"He wants me to help him pick it out." Zoe watched closely, hoping her mom would come out of the place she'd disappeared to.

Her mother looked down at her book.

Together they struggled to converse with her mother for the next fifteen minutes. Her memory came and went all the while. When Zoe became frustrated, Gabe stepped in. She admired his patience. More than once her mom had asked what his name was and each time he'd clearly and calmly told her. Finally, her mother showed signs of frustration.

With a heavy heart, Zoe said, "Mom, it's time for us to go." She kissed her mother's soft cheek, straightened, hoping her mom would say goodbye. All she got was a vaguely puzzled smile. Gabe followed her out of the room, softly closing the door behind him.

As they walked down the hall on their way out, he took her hand. "I know how increasingly difficult visiting her is for you."

Zoe blinked back tears. "It is. I hate that she's losing her memory in general, but I know soon it will be to the point that she'll stop recognizing me altogether." She laid her hand over her middle. "She'll never really know her grandchild. The baby won't know her."

"Then you'll just have to make a special point to tell him or her about your mother." Gabe stepped ahead of her and held open the front door.

"You make it sound so easy." Zoe stepped past him.

"Never said that. My mom never talked about my father much. I wished she had. I don't feel like I know him."

She had a father who had decided he didn't want her. Zoe wasn't sure which was worse—never having a father to begin with, or having one who didn't want you. "My father left us when I was ten. He went to work one day and didn't return."

"I'm sorry. That must have been awful."

Her chest tightened. "It was bad but at least I had him for a little while. The worst is knowing it was that easy to walk away from us."

"Sounds like both of us might have father issues. Not a great thing to have in common, but something." There was sadness in his voice.

"I guess you're right." She looked at him. "Thanks for coming with me." Somehow Gabe's supportive presence had made it easier. She was starting to depend on him. That mistake she had to constantly guard against. He hadn't made any promises to her. He could be gone just as easily as her father, but Gabe was there for her right now.

"You're welcome," he was saying. "I'm glad to see your mom has a quality place to live. You're doing the right thing."

"Then why do I feel so rotten about it?"

Gabe stopped her. Waited until she looked at him before he said, "Because you can't do anything to make the situation better."

She nodded. "I guess."

They arrived at the car.

"So where should we go for this furniture? You're the person who knows the area." Gabe unlocked the doors.

After a minute Zoe answered, "I guess Abrams Furniture is the best place to start. It's the biggest furniture store in the area. Turn left out of the parking lot."

Thirty minutes later, Gabe parked in front of the entrance to the large building with windows showcasing furniture for many different rooms of a house. Gabe held the glass door open for Zoe to enter.

They were quickly greeted by a middle-aged woman. "Hello. What may I show you today?"

Gabe smiled. "We'd like to look at patio furniture."

The lady was quick to return his smile. "Come this way. I'm sure we have something you'll like."

They followed her along a path leading through groupings of sofas and chairs, then dining-room suites, toward the back of the store. The smell of new furniture and polished wood was nearly overpowering. Along the way they passed the nursery section. Before Zoe was the most perfect white crib. Beside it stood a matching chest of drawers, changing table and even a rocker.

She stopped, unable to resist running her fingers along the top of one side of the crib. The image of pastel ruffled drapes on the windows as the sun beamed in filled her mind. A white rocker sat nearby. When she had her own place this would be what she'd like to have for the baby. She was so mesmerized by the pictures in her head, she had to hurry to catch up with Gabe. He waited by a door leading to the outside.

"Did you find something you like?" he asked as she walked by him.

Zoe shook her head. He was already more involved in her life than she had intended to allow. She wasn't going to open her heart to another man who didn't share her dream of commitment and marriage. Heart still healing from her failed relationship with her ex, she certainly wouldn't repeat it when she already knew how Gabe felt.

The woman was waiting for them in the middle of the large covered area. There were all kinds of chairs and tables suitable for outdoor use. Some had metal frames while others were made of wicker. Many appeared nice enough for inside use. There were numerous cushions, in every color choice, both in floral prints and plain fabric. The space was almost overwhelming.

"What do you think would be best on the patio?" Gabe asked her.

"Oh, I don't know. There's so much here. Let me look

around some." She shouldn't be making these types of decisions with him. She wouldn't be staying at his home long. Furniture implied longevity, and that she wouldn't have.

Gabe walked around from one grouping to another. She joined him, making her own path through the jumble.

She wasn't sure what was best for him, but she did know what she liked. "I prefer the wicker look."

"Then that's what we should look at," he said as if pleased.

His attention turned to the saleswoman, who was swift to direct them toward a space with nothing but that style of outdoor furniture. A particular suite caught Zoe's attention. It included a table with a large orange umbrella and four black chairs. Next to them were a matching two-person settee, a lounger, and two chairs with orange cushions and a low table situated between them. The entire set was perfect for Gabe's patio. Classical, yet functional. Zoe headed straight for it.

"Why don't you have a seat and see how it feels?" the saleslady suggested. "See how comfortable it is."

Zoe took a seat in one of the chairs at the table. Gabe sank into an armchair with high sides. It accommodated his large body as if tailor made for him.

"So what do you think?" Gabe looked at her.

"I like this chair. It's sturdy enough, which you'll need if it's going to be outside all the time. But do you really need all of this?" Zoe waved her hand in a circle.

He shrugged. "I have plenty of room for it, so why not? Come try the lounger. You'd use it more than me."

She lowered her voice so the saleswoman couldn't easily hear. "I'm not going to use it that long."

"Please just try the lounger and tell me what you think." There was a pleading note in his voice.

The saleslady must have picked up on it as well because she said, "I'm going to let you two discuss this. If you need me I'll be right over there." She pointed toward the door through which they had exited.

With some annoyance Zoe sat on the lounger, pushed back until she was comfy and put up her legs. It would be the perfect place to read a book, feed their baby. *Their* baby. When had she started thinking of the baby as theirs instead of hers? She glanced at Gabe, shaken on a disturbing level. How did he think of the baby?

She had to stand. Those thoughts weren't ones she needed to have. Heartache, disappointment and disagreement were all they would bring between her and Gabe. Zoe shifted on the cushion, moving to get off it.

Gabe quickly rose and offered her a hand. "So what do you think?"

"It's very nice," she murmured.

He raised a brow in question. "Should I get it?"

Though reluctant to do so, Zoe nodded. "I think so."

"Now, that wasn't so hard, was it?"

She was grateful he didn't give her time to respond before he walked off toward the saleslady.

If Gabe furnished the rest of the house as nicely as the patio, their child would have an amazing place to visit. She wouldn't have to worry about the baby having what he or she needed. Gabe would see to it. In fact, he was quite willing to let her see to it, but she mustn't give in to that temptation. It would be too easy to think and act as if Gabe's house was hers as well and, worse, as if he was.

Gabe was kind, caring and generous. He'd be a good father based on that. Even if he didn't think so. A child deserved both a mother and father in their life. As long as she and Gabe could agree on how the baby should be raised, he or she should have a good life. Not the perfect one like Zoe dreamed of, but a good one nonetheless. What

they had to do was remain civil. When their emotions became involved that was when heartache and anger would
take over and create strife. She couldn't let that happen.

Zoe followed Gabe and the saleswoman into the building. As they walked past the nursery furniture, she made
a point not to look at it, sighing. It would be nice to bring
the baby home from the hospital to a finished nursery, but
that wasn't the plan. When the time was right she'd set one
up. Until then, she'd settle for a cradle in her bedroom.

She joined Gabe at the counter where he'd just finished
paying for the furniture.

"All done." Gabe turned to her with a pleased smile.
"Thanks for your help."

The saleslady said as they headed out the door, "It has
been a pleasure to help such a nice couple."

Zoe's heart caught. A warm feeling raced through her.
She looked at Gabe. Was there any chance that one day
that could be true? He was an honorable and steadfast person. Just the type of man she'd been looking for...

She started to correct the woman, but Gabe placed a
hand at her back and said without missing a beat, "Thanks
for your help." To Zoe he said, "How about an early lunch
before we head home?"

Gabe settled onto a metal chair on the patio of a local
restaurant after seeing Zoe properly seated. The sky was
bright and there was a slight breeze, making it comfortable outside. They had both ordered a sandwich, chips and
a drink. He'd carried it to the table on a tray, thoroughly
delighted with their morning together.

Visiting her mother had been difficult for Zoe and he
was glad he could be there for her. Shopping, even for
something as mundane as furniture, wasn't high on his
list of fun things to do but he'd enjoyed the trip with Zoe.

The only catch in the morning had been when she'd resisted sitting on the lounger. She was using the fact she wasn't going to live at his house long as an excuse to avoid taking any interest in it. He wanted her to feel comfortable while she was there. To his amazement he was in no hurry for her to do so. He would miss her.

Zoe captured his attention when she said, "This is one of those places I've always wanted to go but have never taken the time."

Her light brown hair glowed in the sunlight. There was a touch of color in her cheeks, giving her a healthy look. "Being pregnant seems to agree with you."

Her look quickly locked with his as her hand moved to her middle. He'd come to expect her to do that anytime the baby was mentioned. "It has been easier than I expected, despite the first few months of morning sickness."

Something close to guilt assaulted him. "I'm sorry."

"It's not your fault."

It had better be. His eyes narrowed. "Who else's would it be?"

"I…uh…only meant there's nothing you could have done about it."

"I was just teasing you." Reaching across the table, he brushed away a stray strand of hair from her cheek with the tip of his index finger. "I know what you meant. I still haven't gotten used to the idea that I'm going to be a father."

"You might need to. It won't be that much longer," she said softly.

"Have you picked out names?" Gabe watched her closely. Would he like them? Would she care? Or ask for his suggestions? She didn't have to.

"I've thought of a few." She picked up a chip.

He watched her closely. "Such as?"

"If it's a boy I'd like to name him either William or Michael."

"Those are both good strong names. My father's name was Gabriel Harold." He didn't miss the slight upturn of her lip at the last name.

Zoe said with a dip of her shoulder and an unsure look, "I like Gabriel."

He grinned. "Not a Harold fan?"

She shook her head. "Not really."

Gabe took a bite of his sandwich. He'd like his child to have a name from his side of the family. But it wasn't a demand he believed he could make. "What about girls' names?"

"I was thinking Laura, Mandy, Maggie. My mother's name is Sandra. I wasn't going to make any real decision until I knew the sex."

"And you'll find that out when?"

She glanced at him. "This week. I have a doctor's appointment on Wednesday. I could have known a few weeks ago but I had to push the ultrasound back because of Mother."

Gabe gave an understanding nod. "What time?"

"What time?" Zoe gave him a quizzical tilt of her head.

"What time are you going for the ultrasound? I'll need to make sure I don't have a surgery scheduled." At her flabbergasted look he added, "I told you I wanted to be there."

"Is that really necessary?"

Why would she care if he went? "Is there any reason I shouldn't be there?"

Zoe didn't look at him. "No, not really, but I can just call you when I'm finished."

"I'd like to be in on the surprise as well." Why did it matter to him that he be there for the actual event?

"Okay." She didn't sound convinced but at least he wasn't going to have to persuade her further.

"You know, I've never lived on this side of the country," Gabe said, picking up his sandwich.

Zoe's face brightened. "You'll love it here. There's so much to see and do. Of course, there's everything in Washington but there are historical homes, battlefields, museums and all the seasonal events."

"Do you go to see those things?"

"I used to stay pretty busy attending concerts and festivals until Mother got worse. I've not got to do much of that in a long time." Sadness filled Zoe's eyes.

"Then maybe we should do some of those things before the baby gets here."

An expectant, hopeful look came over her face. He had her full attention. "Would you have time?"

Would he? He had no idea. "I could try."

"I'm sorry. That wasn't a fair question. I know you're busy."

He'd disappointed her. Just as he had other women he'd been interested in. Except it really bothered him that it was happening again with Zoe. There just wasn't much time in his life for extracurricular activities. He wasn't being fair to Zoe to suggest there was. He wanted to make her happy. Maybe he could work something out in a few weeks. He checked his watch. "I'd better get you home. I'm due at the hospital."

"I'm ready." She stood and pushed the chair in.

She didn't say much on the trip home. He pulled up to the front door. "The deliverymen said they could be here today at three. Will you be around?"

"Yes."

"Great. Do you mind seeing that they get the furniture in place?"

"I can take care of it." Zoe climbed out of the car. "Thanks for lunch and going with me to see Mom."

"No problem. See you later."

The doorbell ringing brought Zoe out of sleep. It took her a few seconds to clear her head enough to get off the bed and head up the hall.

She hadn't been surprised when Gabe hadn't even gotten out of the car before he'd left for the hospital. For a moment at lunch she'd hoped that what he said might be different from what he felt. That he would take time for himself. Do something other than work. Then maybe they could do some touristy things together, but as quickly as the hope flickered it had been snuffed out.

Part of knowing Gabe was accepting those types of things weren't high on his priority list. She, on the other hand, believed they were important for a balanced and happy life. With that in mind, she wanted to make the most of the beautiful day, so she took a walk around the neighborhood before settling in for an afternoon nap. She'd forgotten all about the furniture being delivered until the bell rang. She opened the front door to find two uniformed men waiting.

"We're here to deliver your furniture. Would you show us where it goes?"

"Through here." Zoe opened the door wider and led the way through the living room to the patio.

The men followed quietly, nodding as they surveyed the area, then left her. Soon they returned with the armchairs.

"Where would you like these?"

Zoe pointed to the area that received the most sun. They returned to the truck. While they were gone Zoe moved the chairs into position. In just a few minutes all the furniture was sitting on the patio. Even the umbrella was in place and up. She turned around and smiled. The floral and striped cushions with the matching colors added interest. The patio looked perfect. Gabe should enjoy using it. If he took the time to appreciate it. Until she moved she planned to make the most of the lounger as often as possible, starting that afternoon.

One of the deliverymen asked, "Where would you like the rest of it to go?"

"What? I didn't know there was any more." She followed him into the house.

He pulled a paper out of his back pocket and studied it. "We have a whole room of nursery furniture that's supposed to come to this address."

Zoe's heart jumped. Gabe had bought nursery furniture? She'd not seen him even look at any. Maybe he'd done it online.

"Oh, okay."

"So where do we put it?" The man sounded as if he was losing patience.

"In here." Zoe showed him the empty front room.

He left again and returned with his partner. They had a chest of drawers in their arms. Zoe's breath caught. It was the chest in the group she'd liked so much.

"Where do you want it?" one man grunted.

Zoe looked around the room for a second, totally disoriented by what was happening. "Uh, over on that wall." She pointed to the space between the window and the door. Still in a daze at what Gabe had done, she watched as the men brought in the rocker and changing table.

Gabe had been paying attention when she'd admired the crib and had even noticed how much she liked the set. Had any man ever been that in tune with her? He may have little time to spare, but when he was with her he was totally present.

On the next trip, the men brought in the pieces of the baby bed. One returned to the truck and came back with a tool bag. In less than thirty minutes the bed was together and the mattress in place.

"Where would you like this?" one of the men asked.

"Catty-corner, between the windows." She pointed to the area.

They did as she requested. Soon Zoe was showing them out. She returned to the nursery, taking a seat in the rocker. Feeling overwhelmed, she looked around the room. It would make a perfect nursery. She imagined the walls decorated and envisioned the drapery for the windows...

A tear ran down her cheek. The room would be so beautiful. But it would never be hers.

Zoe didn't have a chance to talk to Gabe about what he'd done because he wasn't home when she went to bed. She couldn't question his commitment to his job. Gabe seemed more than willing to put in the hours required. He'd earned her respect for that alone, but then, there was much to admire about Gabe. Too much for her comfort.

Midmorning the next day she was sitting on the patio, reading a book, when the sound of footsteps on the bricks drew her notice.

A moment later Gabe joined her with a glass in his hand. After placing the drink on the low table, he dropped into one of the chairs facing her. "Mornin'. Mind if I join you?"

It was his home. Gabe didn't have to ask her. "Sure."

She stared at him. Every feminine cell in her body stood at attention and tingled. He acted rested and relaxed. His hair was still damp and tousled as if he'd dried it with a towel and done nothing more to it after his shower. A T-shirt fit close to his chest and his jeans were well-worn with holes in the knees. He was gorgeous.

As if unaware of her admiration, he placed his feet on the table, crossed his ankles and leaned back in the chair.

"It looks great out here. I like the way you arranged everything."

Zoe was pleased by his praise. Too much so. "I'm glad you do. I didn't know how you would want it."

"I had no doubt I could trust you." He grinned.

"Why didn't you tell me that you were buying nursery furniture?"

He pursed his lips and shrugged. "Maybe because I thought you might argue with me about it. I needed something for the baby anyway. You don't like it?"

"I like it very much."

A smug look covered his face. "I thought you might. I saw you looking at it."

He had noticed her interest. She confessed, "I was thinking about getting it for the nursery at my place."

"Why don't you fix up the room the way you like it? You can take it all with you when you go. I'll get more furniture."

"I couldn't do that."

"Sure you can. The baby'll be coming home to this house. He or she needs their own space. Wouldn't it be nice for it to have some continuity from here to your house?"

That really wasn't necessary but Zoe liked the idea of having a special place for the baby from the beginning. "I had planned to just use a cradle for the few weeks I'm still here. I'll think about finishing the nursery."

Gabe picked up his glass, took a long draw on the iced tea and set it down again. "Good. I promised I'd come up with a figure for your rent. But before I give you that I'd like you to consider a proposition."

Her heart leaped. Proposition? What kind of proposition?

"I've been thinking, and don't want to offend you, but you've been cooking meals, even doing some shopping, and I appreciate you have your own job to deal with, but I've not had time to find a housekeeper. If you'd be willing, and thought you had time, to just keep things straightened around here for a little while, then I would forgo the rent altogether. I don't want to imply that I think you should be my housekeeper or anything…"

Zoe hadn't expected this. The extra money she would save would make a nice down payment on the house she wanted. She enjoyed cooking and was doing that for herself anyway. The housekeeping wouldn't be that much. Gabe wasn't home long enough to get anything dirty. Plus, he was neat. She was already taking care of her side of the house. "I think that would work."

"Excellent." He stood. "Then I'm going to catch up on some reading and watch the ball game."

"Okay. I'll make lunch in a little while."

"Sounds great." He strolled to the house.

They were acting like a married couple on Sunday afternoon now. It should have made her feel uneasy but instead there was a satisfaction there, contentment. She looked into the living area at Gabe. He was sitting in his chair with his legs stretched out and his attention on the TV. Wouldn't it be nice if it was always this way between them? It was a wonderful dream. But just a dream. Gabe had never mentioned his feelings regarding her. He was a decent man but that didn't mean he cared for her the way Zoe wanted him to.

CHAPTER SEVEN

GABE STUDIED ZOE. She'd been reading for the last couple of hours while he had supposedly watched TV. Even though he wasn't outside with her, he was very aware of her movements. From his chair he could see her better than she could him. Was she aware of how many times her hand went to the rounded area of her stomach? Just from that small action he had no doubt she loved and wanted their baby.

Her gaze met his through the glass. She gave him a small smile before she returned to her reading. Only by a force of will did he stop himself from getting up and going out to kiss her. Or more. But he'd promised not to touch her again unless she initiated it. He would keep his promise even if it killed him.

Sometime later Zoe came in and quietly went to the kitchen. Now he was listening to her moving around as she prepared a late lunch. Something about having her in his home, being around her, sharing meals and even picking out furniture seemed right. She brought a softness to his life that he hadn't known he had been missing. Did he want to let it go? Was he capable of hanging on to it?

Would Zoe consider staying if he asked? They got along well. But she wanted a husband. Could he offer her that? Be the husband she needed? What if he didn't measure up to her expectations? Could he even be the father to his child that he should be? How would he ever know? He'd had no firsthand experience, not seen a father in action close-up. Could he find enough balance in his life to make it work? Which would be worse: not taking the chance or failing?

Zoe brought him a plate with a sandwich and salad on it.

"Thank you."

She smiled. "You're welcome." She continued outside to the table.

He watched her. She hadn't invited him to join her. Would she mind if he did? One of the things he liked most about having Zoe in the house was sharing meals and conversation.

Taking his plate, he went to join her. Zoe didn't look up as he approached. He'd like to know her thoughts. "Do you mind?"

Her head jerked around. "Uh, sure. It's your patio."

Annoyance ran hot through him. "I wish you'd quit thinking like that. This is your home for as long as you stay. I want you to treat it that way."

"I'll try."

"Don't try. Accept it." He took a chair beside her.

She pushed a leaf of lettuce around on her plate. "It just seems strange to live with someone you know so little about."

"What do you want to know?" He bit into his sandwich. Was it so good because of the sliced ham and cheese or because Zoe had made it?

"I don't know," she said slowly, as if giving it thought. "What's your favorite color?"

"Green." *Like your eyes*, but he didn't say that. "What's yours?"

"Red. But I'm supposed to be asking you questions."

He grinned. "Ever think I might like to learn a few things about you?"

"Okay, then. Do you like a dog or a cat?"

"Dog. Big dog. And you?" He looked up from the fork he was filling with salad and raised a brow in question.

"I always wanted a Labrador retriever but didn't have a good place for one to live." A dreamy look came over her face.

"Nice dogs. Good with children, I've heard."

She focused on him again. "Favorite vacation spot?"

"I like the beach but the mountains are nice too. What I like is to be active and learn something wherever I go."

"Learn something?" She pulled her sandwich apart and took the cheese off it.

"Yeah, I like taking trips centered around a subject where there are lectures and visits to places where events happened. History, social service, medical missions."

Zoe nibbled at the cheese and then said, "I haven't done that. Maybe I've been missing out on something." She paused in a pensive manner before asking, "Where have you been on a medical mission?"

"I've made a couple of trips to South America, another to Arizona."

"Oh!" Zoe jumped.

Gabe leaned forward, concern making him study her. "What's wrong? You hurt somewhere?"

Her smile turned to a sweet, reflective one. "The baby kicked."

He looked to where her hand rested. Despite being a doctor, the action filled him with awe.

She hissed and looked at him. "There it was again."

"May I feel?" he asked softly. The need to know the small life growing in her would take him to his knees, begging, if that was what it took to get her to agree.

She nodded. He placed his hand where hers had been.

There was nothing. Zoe flinched again but he didn't feel anything. Placing her hand over the top of his, she moved it slightly and pressed. A second later there was a thump against his palm. His gaze snapped to meet hers. At that moment she took his heart.

He leaned forward with the intention of kissing her. But he'd promised. "Zoe…"

She wanted and deserved assurances he wasn't prepared to give. He needed space. Gabe stood and picked up his plate. "Thanks for sharing that with me."

Zoe looked at him with big wide eyes before he stalked away.

Fifteen minutes later he was on his way to the hospital.

Wednesday morning Zoe sat in the obstetrician's office, waiting for the nurse to call her name. She'd not seen Gabe since Sunday afternoon. He'd been gone Monday by the time she'd gone to the kitchen. She'd heard him come in once but it had been late and she'd already been in bed.

His new job might be demanding but the thought had crossed her mind that maybe he was dodging her. She wasn't sure why he would be but something about the way he'd abruptly left on Sunday made her question his actions.

She'd texted him the time of the appointment and the address. Maybe he'd changed his mind about being there. She wasn't sure how she felt about that. His insistence had taken her by surprise. Although she knew she shouldn't, she wanted to share the moment of discovery with him.

A nurse standing at the door leading back to the examination rooms called Zoe's name. She searched the entrance to the outside of the building as disappointment filled her. Apparently Gabe wasn't coming. After all he'd said about being involved and the one time she'd agreed, he wasn't taking advantage of it. She'd let herself believe… What, she wasn't sure. That there might be a chance for them?

That Gabe could really care about the baby beyond being honorable? Or that he could want to be there for her? All of it was just wishful thinking. Nothing based on reality.

She followed the nurse back to the examination room. Inside she sat on the table with shoulders slumped and waited. Her situation with Gabe reminded her of her relationship with Shawn and her father. She hadn't been able to depend on them. They were unreliable, would hurt her. She saw it one way when in reality it was all another. With Gabe she needed to keep what was truth separated from wishful thinking.

Zoe had been waiting a few minutes when there was a quick rap on the door. Fully expecting the doctor, she was shocked to see Gabe step in. She couldn't deny the joy surging into her chest. He had come.

"I'm sorry I'm late. I got tied up at the last minute," he said, puffing as if he'd been running. He came to stand beside her. "Have I missed anything?"

His breathless enthusiasm made her smile. He was acting like a kid looking for a piece of candy. "No. The doctor hasn't been in yet."

"Good." He sank into the only chair in the room.

Moments later the door opened and this time it was her doctor. He gave Gabe a questioning once-over.

Gabe stood and offered his hand. "Gabe Marks. I'm the baby's father."

Zoe didn't miss the proud tone of his voice. Another gentle wave of happiness washed over her.

"Nice to meet you," the doctor said, then turned to her. "This visit is the one where we do the anatomy ultrasound. The question is, do you want to know the sex?"

Before Zoe could speak Gabe said, "I'm more interested in knowing if Zoe and baby are all right."

Tears sprang to Zoe's eyes. She'd not expected that statement.

"That I can let you know as well, but I don't anticipate a problem with either one of them." The doctor smiled at her.

"That's good to hear," Gabe said, then looked at her. "We do want to know the sex, don't we?"

Zoe nodded.

"Okay," her doctor said. "The tech will be in in a few minutes to do the ultrasound. Then I'll be back to do the examination." That said, he left, closing the door behind him.

"Are you okay?" Gabe asked now that they were alone.

"Yeah. Why?"

"You just had a funny look on your face a few minutes ago." Either she'd revealed too much or he'd been watching her too closely.

"I'm just excited."

Gabe took her hand. "I know this wasn't what either of us planned, but I have to admit that bringing a new life into the world is pretty amazing." He kissed her forehead.

The tenderness of the moment dissolved when there was another knock at the door, but the lingering contentment would last a long time.

Gabe held the door open for the tech, who was pushing a large machine on wheels. "Hi, I'm Sarah. I'll be doing your ultrasound." She positioned the machine beside the exam table. "Are you Dad?" she asked Gabe.

"Yes."

"Then what I'd like you to do is sit in the chair until I get everything all set up. Then you can come and stand beside Mom." She started getting the cables organized.

A perplexed look came over Gabe's face. Zoe couldn't help but grin. Her guess was that Gabe did most of the ordering in his world and to have this woman in control of the situation had to go against the grain. Despite that, he did what the tech requested but watched her with narrowed eyes.

"Let's get you further up on the table." The woman helped Zoe scoot back. "Now, please pull up your shirt."

Zoe did, revealing the roundness of her belly, made more pronounced by lying down. She looked over at Gabe. His attention was fixed on her middle. There was something telling and intense about his focus. Seconds later his gaze rose to meet hers and his eyes softened. What was he thinking?

Soon the tech squirted a glob of gel on Zoe's belly and had the transducer moving over her skin. The swishing sound of the baby's heart beating filled the room. "Okay, Dad, you can come and stand beside Mom."

Gabe didn't have to be asked twice. When he was beside her, he placed his hand over hers where it rested on the exam table, curling his fingers into her palm. It was as if he had to be touching her. For a man who had asserted he didn't have time or room in his life for a family, he seemed very interested in her and this baby. Maybe he didn't know what he really wanted.

The tech continued to watch the screen as she moved the transducer over Zoe. "All right, I understand you want to know what gender this baby is. Let's see if we can find out."

Zoe glanced at Gabe. He was watching the screen intently.

Before Zoe could look back the tech said, "I believe with that anatomy it's a boy."

Pure joy filled Gabe's face. He squeezed her hand and breathed softly, "A boy."

Zoe looked at the screen. There was their baby boy. Would he look like Gabe? She hoped so. Tall, dark-haired with magnetic blue eyes. What child could go wrong with that combination?

A ringing sound had Gabe letting go of her hand and digging into his pocket. He looked at the cell phone and stepped away from her. Just that quickly the special moment evaporated.

"Dr. Marks." He listened then said, "I'll be right there." He ended the connection and considered her, his face grave. "I have to go. I have to be there to supervise."

His mind was already somewhere else.

"I know." Zoe did understand. She was glad that at least he'd made it there for their special moment.

He moved around the machine and slipped out the door.

Zoe watched it close between them. It was just one more reminder nothing had changed and she shouldn't get her hopes up.

Gabe would have never thought he'd be this absorbed in a baby. Was it because the child was his or because Zoe was carrying it? Or both? There had always been an attraction between him and Zoe, but in the last few weeks it had grown into something more. A feeling he didn't want to put a name to or analyze, but that was taking control nonetheless.

He'd hated to leave her so abruptly, especially after his almost too late arrival. They had shared one of the most surreal moments of his life. He had been watching his son on the screen. More than that, he'd shared it with Zoe. For heaven's sake, he was a physician and he'd gone through the OB rotation in medical school, but this time it was his child.

Although it was late in the evening before he headed out of the hospital, he still had a stop to make. Less than an hour later he pulled into the garage beside Zoe's car. With a smile on his face, he picked up the brown bag in the passenger seat and climbed out of the car. Would Zoe think his purchase was silly or give him an understanding smile? It didn't matter which, because he'd been unable to help himself.

There was a light burning in the kitchen but no Zoe. With the bag in his hand, he went to her hallway. "Zoe." There was no answer. He took a few more steps toward her room. "Zoe?"

Seconds later the sound of music playing met his ears. She must not be able to hear him. He went to her bedroom door. "Zoe." Still nothing. Now he was getting worried. Had she passed out? Fallen in the shower?

He stepped to the bathroom door and jerked to a stop. His throat tightened and his heart pounded. Zoe stood in front of the large mirror over the sink. She had her night-gown pulled up to below her breasts and was looking down while her hands slowly roamed over her expanded middle. A serene smile of wonderment lit her lovely face.

Gabe shifted.

Her head whipped toward him, her eyes wide. She reached for her gown.

"Please, don't." His words were soft and beseeching. "You're so beautiful. Breathtaking."

Zoe's hands stilled but she watched him with unmis-takable wariness.

Gabe placed the bag on the counter and slowly stepped behind her. Their gazes locked in the mirror. There was a question in her eyes. His arms circled her. She trembled when his palms touched her warm, smooth skin. Would she push him away?

His heart thundered in his ears when her hands cov-ered his, her fingers interlacing with his. She moved them down and around until they cupped the tight globe en-casing their baby. Zoe closed her eyes and leaned back against him. Gabe had never seen her look more angelic. Inhaling, he took in the soft, subtle scent of her freshness. He could do nothing more than stare. What he had in his arms was precious.

She once again moved his hands to rest at what had

once been the curve of her hips. There was a small push against one of his palms. Gabe hissed. His heart swelled. Emotions too strong to comprehend grew in his chest and spread out to overtake him. This was territory he'd never been to before. "Zoe, thank you."

Zoe stood perfectly still. Gabe's voice was like a tender kiss upon her neck. She opened her eyes, meeting his intense, passionate gaze. He'd said he wouldn't touch her again unless she asked him to, so it was up to her to make the first move. Turning in his arms, she wrapped her arms around his neck and pushed up on her toes. Her lips lightly touched his. "No. Thank you."

Gabe's mouth pressed into hers, igniting that fire that only he could. He pulled her closer. His lips slid over hers, leaving sweet waves of sensation radiating out through her body. She put her fingers to the hair at the nape of his neck, ran them through it. Moments later, Gabe's gentle touch traveled over her back, grasping and releasing as his arms circled her, lifting her against him. She went willingly.

Where their previous kisses had been frantic, this one was loving and exploring, wondering and appreciating. Zoe moaned and melted further into him. She was sure she wasn't taking the most rational action, but she could no longer fight her emotions.

Gabe's mouth left hers to skim along her cheek, leaving small caresses that held more reverence than passion. He kissed her temple then the shell of her ear. "I want you. Just to hold you."

"I want that too," she purred against his lips.

Releasing her, Gabe lowered the gown covering her. He took her hand, leading her out of the bathroom and across the house toward his room. Zoe had resisted going into his space. Had even put off cleaning there. Something about it was just too intimate. Now she was being invited in. Wanted.

Gabe let go of her hand at the door, moving into the dark room alone. Seconds later, a small lamp on a bureau lit the space. Gabe's furniture was massive. It suited him. The king-size bed was the centerpiece with its dark green spread. On either side were two end tables. At one end of the room was a fireplace with enough space for a sitting area, but there was nothing there.

He returned to her, offering his hand. Zoe took it. She wanted this. Needed the closeness. Gabe led her to the bedside. His blue eyes seemed to glow with emotion. She was unable to identify which one before his lips found hers. His mouth touched hers gently, giving instead of taking. It was as if he was trying to convey his feelings without voicing them.

For the first time Zoe dared to hope that there might be a future for them.

When Gabe pulled away, he gave her another searching look. Going down on one knee, he took the hem of her gown and rolled it up. She sucked in a breath. With her heart in her throat, Zoe watched him lean in and place a kiss where their baby grew. Gabe turned his head, placing his cheek against her. Her hand cradled his head and held him close. Moisture filled her eyes.

He rose, bringing the gown up with him. Seconds later he stripped it off over her head. She shivered, her arms instantly covering her breasts.

"Please don't hide from me. You're stunning." Gabe knelt and slowly slipped her panties to her feet.

Zoe stepped out of them as he pulled the bedspread back. Gabe turned and swept her up against his chest. One of her arms went around his shoulders as she buried her face in his neck, her mouth finding heated skin. He worshipfully placed her between the sheets then stood gazing down at her as if memorizing each curve and dip.

"You're so beautiful. I just don't have the words."

Zoe's heart danced. She lifted her arms, inviting him to join her. Gabe sat beside her instead. Their gazes held as he placed a hand over the baby. Hers came to rest on his before he slowly leaned down to kiss her. His sweet, tender ways were her undoing. This was the affection that love was made of. In her heart she'd known it when she'd invited him into her hotel room that fateful stormy night. Cupping his face in both hands, she held his mouth to hers.

His kisses were easy, caring, loving. She was being cherished with each touch of his lips. He controlled their kiss, refusing when she wanted to take it deeper. Her soul played joyous notes as he lightly skimmed his mouth over hers.

Zoe sucked in a breath as his attention left her lips to travel over her cheek. His mouth found the sweet spot behind her ear, pressed and suckled. His fingertips trailed down along the length of her arm and up again. She shuddered. Every nerve in her body was alive where Gabe's next touch landed. He moved to her shoulder, leaving a kiss in the dip there before dropping more along a path to the rise of her breast.

Her breath hitched then caught when he cradled her in his hand. He shifted her breast, looked for a second before his mouth covered her nipple. Fireworks went off inside her, her breasts grew heavy, and her core tingled. Her fingers funneled into his hair as she relaxed on the pillow, closed her eyes and took in each precious nuance of his caresses.

"Gabe." She lifted her shoulders, tugging his head toward hers.

He resisted. "Shh. Just feel."

Could she take more? That was all she was doing—feeling. Her body was on fire with want. Her body throbbed, ached, begged for relief.

Gabe suckled then circled her nipple with his tongue. Her body clenched. As he continued to worship her with his mouth, his hand traveled tantalizingly slow over her hip then across her middle. A finger traced the circumference of her belly button before it glided downward. It brushed her curls and Zoe's hips flexed. Gabe kissed the baby once more before his mouth returned to cover hers.

He pulled away too soon and she groaned, reaching for him in protest. Gabe chuckled lightly as he shifted on the bed so that her calves lay across his lap. The firm bulge of his manhood was visible beneath his pants. A slight smile came to her lips. He hadn't remained unaffected by their kisses.

Zoe watched as he picked up her foot and began to massage it. When she pulled at a corner of the sheet in an effort to cover herself, he tugged it away.

"I want to admire you. Watch your body turn all rosy for me."

She'd never lain naked in front of a man, much less while he touched and kissed her all over. There was something titillating and erotic about it to be desired so.

Gabe paid special attention to each of her toes, pulling gently before moving to the next. When he was done, he brought her foot to his mouth and placed his lips to her arch. Zoe sighed. This was heaven. How it should be between a man and a woman. Their gazes met and held. She bit her bottom lip as Gabe slowly ran his hand from her ankle up to her thigh, slipped inside the crease of her legs and then moved down again.

How much longer could she take his ministrations?

His wicked smile was equally sexy as he picked up her other foot. Confidence covered his handsome face. He was aware of what he was making her feel, enjoying it. After giving that foot the same attention he had given the other, he grabbed a pillow, placed it beside her, then another and did the same before he said, "Turn over."

"Gabe, I don't think—"

"Trust me."

In spite of all her precautions, she'd found she could do just that. Gabe was so much more than she'd first given him credit for. Rolling not very gracefully onto her stomach, she allowed Gabe to help place the pillows so that any pressure was off the baby. She glanced back to see he had moved again so that he sat beside her hips. Over the next few minutes she concentrated on the provocative feel of his fingers as they teased their way up one leg, slipped between it and the other long enough for her center to burn with need, before moving away, leaving her wanting. Too soon his hand moved on to the other leg, teasing her to the point she quivered all over. When she believed Gabe could do nothing more to raise her arousal higher, his mouth found the curve of her back. His lips kissed their way up her back one vertebra at a time. At her neck, he pushed her hair away and gave her a sensual nip as his hand brushed the side of her breast. Zoe groaned.

"Roll to your back." Gabe's voice was gruff as if he were grasping for control. She couldn't have moved without his help. Gabe's magic hands had reduced her to nothing more than a lump of putty held together by bones. When she'd returned to her back, his attentions went directly to the V of her legs, touching, withdrawing and approaching to tease once again.

"I want to watch you find your pleasure." His voice was low, coaxing. His lips settled on hers as his finger slipped into her center. She jerked upward, eager for relief only Gabe could provide.

His mouth slowly released hers before his look captured hers, held. He moved his finger faster. Tension built in her, squeezed, pulsed, before the dam burst. Her eyes widened as she flew off into paradise. She saw the look of wonder on Gabe's face as she shuddered before her eyelids fluttered closed.

"Thank you," she murmured.

He kissed her forehead. "My pleasure, honey."

CHAPTER EIGHT

GABE'S FINGERS TRAILED across Zoe's shoulder as he pulled back and stood. He covered her. What he'd experienced with Zoe had never happened to him before. He had always thought of himself as a generous lover and seen to his partner's release, but he'd never given anyone the attention he had given her. He'd not worried about his own desires but hers instead, determined that Zoe understood all he felt.

She was special. Very. If she was willing, he wanted to work something out. Find a way they could stay together after the baby. When the time was right he would talk to her about it. See if she felt the same way. But still he worried he couldn't give her all she wanted. Could he be that present husband and father she dreamed of? Was he willing to find the balance in his life that would make it work?

He headed for the shower. It would be a cold one tonight. Sometime later he turned off the lamp and crawled under the bedcovers, pulling the warm, sleeping Zoe to him. With a sigh he drifted off to sleep. This was too right.

It was still dark when Zoe's warm bottom rubbed against him. In an instant his body responded.

"Mmm..." Zoe murmured, before she turned to face him, her hand resting on his chest.

Gabe wasn't sure she was awake but he certainly was.

Zoe slid her hand up his chest and behind his neck. When she kissed his chest he sucked in a breath.

"You awake?" Her sleep-laden voice sounded so sexy.

"Yes, honey. I'm awake." And in pain.

"Honey." She kissed his chest again. "I like it when you call me that."

Gabe brushed his hand over the lower part of her back. He'd never called a woman that before.

"I like it," Zoe mumbled. "And I like you."

"I like you too." His lips found hers.

She pulled closer, moving and shifting so the baby pressed more into his side than on his middle. Her mouth opened for him. Gabe took her invitation. His tongue found hers, performing an erotic dance that was theirs alone.

"If you continue that, I won't keep my promise to just hold you."

"I'd like being held but I like other things too." Her hand moved lower.

"Are you sure?" If she continued, he would do anything she asked.

Zoe pulled his face to hers, kissing his eyes, his cheek, his chin before her lips found his. She squirmed, brushing against his arousal. That was more than Gabe could take. He rolled Zoe to her back and braced himself over her on his hands.

Gently, he entered her. Zoe lifted her hips, helping him to settle deep in her. As he entered and withdrew in the age-old manner, Zoe hissed while her fingers gripped his shoulders as he moved. His lips found hers. He increased the pace. She squirmed beneath him as if trying to work closer. With uncertain control, he built their pleasure until Zoe moaned and the tension in her relaxed. Gabe thrust a few more times, before he groaned his release. He fell to Zoe's side and pulled her close, kissing her shoulder. Would life ever be this good again…?

The buzzing of his phone woke him. He was needed at the hospital. Only hazy sunlight was coming through the windows when he slid out of bed. Minutes later he was ready to leave when he leaned over and kissed the still sleeping Zoe. He wanted to climb back in beside her but he was being pulled away. He took a moment to watch her. Would it always be this way for him? Leaving her behind? What was he allowing to happen? If he could stop it, would he?

But what would he have missed if Zoe hadn't come into his life?

With the tip of his finger, he pushed a stray lock of hair off her cheek and forced himself to walk out of the room.

Zoe woke to cool sheets beside her, but the hot memories of the night before had her whole body still tingling. The room was bright with light. She jerked to a sitting position. Apparently she had overslept. She didn't ever do that. Making her way to her room for her phone, she called in and told the office she would be in soon.

She stepped into the bath and saw the bag sitting on the counter. Unable to resist, she peeked inside. A smile spread across her face. How like a man. Not wanting to spoil Gabe's surprise, she took the bag to the kitchen and placed it on the table. On the counter, she found a note.

Honey, I'll bring dinner home.

Honey. The word was like golden sunshine on a cloudy morning.

Zoe went through the day with a smile on her face. More than one person at her office commented on how happy she looked. She just smiled and kept her reason to herself. Saying why might make it disappear, and even if she did, what could she say? That she was in love with a man she wasn't sure was in love with her. Their relationship wasn't any more secure than it had been before. With her past, she'd learned the bitter lesson that not everything was always the way it appeared.

Gabe invaded her thoughts in every spare moment. Had they turned a corner where things would be different between them? Could they, would they find a future? Did Gabe want to? The baby was a life-changing event in their lives and she couldn't help but hope last night had been as well.

He'd given so completely, been so tender and caring during their lovemaking. There had been none of the frenzy of their first time, but the experience had been just as satisfying. The night had included passion but it had been wrapped in caring, sharing, getting to know each other on a level like never before. Had Gabe been expressing his feelings through his actions?

She could only hope. Yet a nagging fear remained that it might go away in the reality of everyday life. Zoe pushed away the negativity, determined to enjoy what they had shared and what she hoped would be between them in the future. She planned to make the most of Gabe's attentions for as long as they lasted, even if it was only for a few months. Her mother's illness and her father's defection had taught her not to take any day for granted. She would grasp all the happiness she could.

It was late afternoon when she arrived home. As she suspected, Gabe wasn't yet there. It was such a nice day and she'd been inside too much of it, so she planned to take a walk around the neighborhood. Zoe had reached the bottom of the driveway when Gabe pulled in.

Her heart fluttered just at the sight of him.

He stopped and rolled down the window. "Hi."

Zoe couldn't help feeling nervous and a little shy. "Hey."

He watched her too closely for her comfort. "What're you up to?"

"I was going for a walk." She shifted from one foot to the other.

Gabe smiled. "Give me a sec and I'll go with you."

She wasn't sure but she was afraid she might have looked at him as if he was from another planet. That had been the last thing she'd expected out of his mouth. "Won't dinner get cold?"

"It'll need to be warmed up anyway."

"Okay." Wasn't this the man who'd said he didn't have time for family? Now he was home early, with dinner in his hand, and he wanted to go for a walk? It was too good to be true.

He continued on up the drive. She walked behind him and waited at the porch while Gabe parked. Zoe watched as he strolled toward her with a sense of pride. Gabe was a tall, handsome male with a swagger of confidence that made him even sexier. The collar of the light blue shirt that matched his eyes was open and the sleeves were rolled up on his forearms. His pants were classic and fit him to perfection. All of this magnificence was hers. Gabe could be any woman's dream, but he was hers to enjoy.

When he reached her, he smiled and took her hand. "So how was your day?"

She was still uncertain around him. After all the emotion of the night before, he seemed so calm when she was still walking as if on clouds. "Good. I stopped by to see Mom on the way home. She's doing about the same. How about yours?"

"The usual—but I do have some news I think you'll like."

She looked at him. "What?"

"The committee agreed to list Mr. Luther."

She grabbed his arm, stopping him. "That's wonderful. Thank you!" She wrapped her arms around his waist and hugged him.

He pulled her close. "None of it was really my doing. The committee all voted yes after the social worker and psychiatrist had spoken to him. He assured them that he'd do what he needed to do."

"Still, you were the one who agreed to see him in the first place." If she had believed him wonderful before, he was her hero now.

"You're welcome."

Gabe was so humble about what he did for other people. Just another reason she was crazy about him.

They continued down the sidewalk, their hands clasped between them.

"You know, I've never taken you for a person who might enjoy a walk around the neighborhood. But I like it that you came with me."

"I can be full of surprises." Gabe squeezed her hand.

He was. Just a few weeks ago she would have sworn this day would never happen.

They walked a couple of blocks and turned around. As they did so, Gabe said, "I called my mother today. Told her we were having a boy. She was excited. Said she was looking forward to meeting you."

What did his mother think about their situation? "I look forward to meeting her too."

That worrying thought was interrupted by someone calling, "Hi."

Zoe looked to see an older couple standing near a manicured flower bed.

She and Gabe stopped.

The balding man, followed by his wife, stepped closer

to the walk. "You must be our newest neighbor. The one who moved into the brick house with the curved drive."

"Yes, sir, that's us," Gabe said, offering his hand to the man. The man took it and they shook. "I'm Gabriel Marks." He put his arm at her waist and said, "And this is Zoe."

The way he left the introduction implied that they were married. Zoe wasn't sure how she felt about that. Had Gabe just not wanted to go into the details of their relationship at a casual meeting?

"I'm Richard Mills, and this is my wife, Maggie."

"It's nice to meet you both," Gabe said.

Maggie stepped closer and smiled. "I see that you're expecting a little one."

Zoe placed her hand on her middle. "Yes. He's due in a couple of months."

"A little boy. How wonderful. We'll need to get the neighbors together and give y'all a baby shower."

"Oh, that's sweet but not necessary." Zoe didn't want to have to go into explaining her and Gabe's relationship. The bubble of happiness she'd had minutes before had popped.

"We could make it a block party and shower. It'd be a wonderful way for everyone to meet each other." Her enthusiasm made her voice higher. "It'd be a lot of fun."

Zoe just smiled.

Maggie continued, "A lot of us who live around here are grandparents but our grandkids are no longer small. To have small children around will be wonderful. Ooh, to get to buy one of those cute little outfits." She all but rubbed her hands together in glee.

Zoe felt like a fraud. This couple thought her and Gabe were a happy couple in the process of becoming a happy family. She wished it was true. But Gabe had said nothing about that happening.

Gabe's smile had turned tight. "We need to head home. We've supper waiting for us."

"Great to meet you," Richard said. "See you soon."

"You too," Gabe said, as they started down the sidewalk.

"They seemed like nice people," Zoe said quietly. "They think we're married."

"Yeah, I suspect they do." Gabe didn't look at her while matching his pace to hers.

What was he thinking? Some of the joy of the day had dimmed. They continued in silence until they were in front of his house. She wanted their earlier camaraderie back. "I enjoyed our walk."

"I did too."

Zoe gave him a suspicious look. "What's happening to you?"

"Uh?"

"I'd have never guessed the always-busy type A doctor would've ever said something like that."

He grinned. "Could be you're a good influence on me."

Did she really have that kind of effect on him?

As they entered the house through the carport door, Gabe said, "I brought us some of the best Italian in town. Or so I've been told. It's from a little restaurant close to the hospital. I'll get it warmed up."

"Then I'm on dish duty." Zoe headed for the kitchen. She'd forgotten about the bag waiting on the table. Picking it up, she held it out. "By the way, you left this in my bathroom last night."

He gave her a wolfish grin. "I had other things on my mind."

Heat warmed her cheeks. She'd had other things on her mind as well.

Gabe took it from her. "You didn't peek, did you?"

She shrugged and tried to look innocent. "Maybe a little."

"Why am I not surprised?" He dug into the bag. "What do you think?" Gabe proudly held up a ball and a tiny baseball glove.

She smiled. "I think it'll be a while before he can use them."

Gabe grinned. "Maybe so but he'll have them when he's ready."

"Yes, he will." But would Gabe be around to play with him? Go to the games?

They worked around each other for the next few minutes. During one of her passes by him, Gabe caught her hand and pulled her to him. "I haven't had one of these in too long." He gave her a tender yet searching kiss.

The insecurity of earlier disappeared, replaced by the bliss of being in his arms again.

His lips left hers. "I could do without a meal to have you again but you need to eat. You tempt me so much."

She tempted him? Had she ever received a more exciting compliment?

After dinner Zoe stood at the sink, washing up the few dishes they had used. Gabe came up behind her. The heat from his body warmed her from shoulders to hips. His arms circled her before he pushed her hair away from her neck and gave her a kiss.

She could get used to this attention. His change in attitude and all his actions were almost surreal but they were everything she had dreamed of having in a husband.

"Forget those and let's go outside and sit for a little while."

Her heart opened more. Even that simple statement made her melt. He wanted to spend time with her. The impression she'd had of him when they'd first met had been that he would never have slowed down long enough to enjoy anything as simple as sitting outside under the stars. Then his life had seemed to center on his career. "Almost done here. You go on and I'll be right there."

Minutes later she wiped her hands off on the dishrag and headed to the patio. Gabe was sitting on the settee with one foot propped on the table. He looked relaxed and content. With his stressful job, he needed downtime. She was glad he could find it.

She moved to take a chair but he grabbed her hand and tugged her toward him. "You'll be too far away if you sit there."

She sat next to him. His arm went around her shoulders, pulling her close.

"This is much better."

Zoe sighed softly. *Much.* The evening sounds of bugs and the occasional bark of a dog joined the sound of Gabe's soft breathing. Could life get better than this? Only if it could be like this forever.

"I've been thinking about a baby name now that we know what it's going to be." She sat so near she could feel the tension of anticipation in Gabe's body. Did he hope the baby would be named after him?

The calm of his voice didn't give anything away. "Have you decided on something?"

"I have."

"Will you tell me?"

"William. Call him Will. What do you think?"

"I like it." The hint of disappointment in his voice didn't escape her.

She couldn't help but tease him, prolonging saying more.

In a huff he asked, "What about the middle name?"

"Well…" She turned so she could see his face. "…I was thinking about Gabriel, after his father and grandfather. What do you think?"

"William Gabriel Marks. That's a fine, strong name."

"Avery. William Gabriel Avery."

He gave her a searching look. Would he argue? He couldn't expect the baby to have his last name if they weren't married. He nodded. Was it acceptance or appeasement?

"Tell me what you know about your daddy. I'd like to know something about Will's heritage."

Gabe didn't like the sour taste in his mouth that came with knowing his boy wouldn't carry his last name. Yet he didn't believe he could demand the name be different. He was well acquainted with Zoe's strong will and determination. She wouldn't easily change her mind. Neither probably should she.

He wasn't sure he was qualified to answer the question about his dad. This wasn't how he would have imagined their romantic moments on the patio going. But then, he'd have never guessed he'd be enjoying an evening like this.

Zoe wouldn't let the question about his father go either. He could only name a few people he'd ever share the story with. "I don't know a lot about him. Like I said, Mother never told me much. I think it's too painful even to this day. He was from Arizona and a teacher. He liked the outdoors. I think my parents had a good marriage but a too short one."

He'd never thought about how deeply his mother must have cared for his father. Had his mother never remarried because she'd missed his father so badly she couldn't bear the hurt of losing another? What would it be like to love that deeply? Could *he*? Did he already?

"That's a shame. It can be hard to find the right person, and when you do, to lose them so…" Zoe's voice trailed off, as though she'd said more than she wanted to.

She must know from experience. Her father had run out on her and she'd lost him, and now for all intents and

purposes her mother was gone as well. She had to understand loss far better than he. Possibly love as well.

"Zoe, if you don't want to answer this I'll understand,
but would you tell me about *your* father?"

She was close enough he felt her body stiffen.

He squeezed her shoulder. "You don't have to talk about
it if you don't want to."

"It doesn't make the hurt any less by not talking about
it. I was crazy about him. He could do no wrong. If he
was at home I was under his feet. I don't know if I just
didn't want to see his unhappiness or I couldn't, but it had
to have been there."

She was too hard on herself. "You were a kid. You
weren't supposed to see."

"I know, but it would have been easier than him just
not coming home one day."

He hugged her again. It would have.

"I asked Mom what happened and all she could say was
that he just wasn't happy. That he had to leave."

"You never saw him again?"

"No. We found out a few years later he had died of an
overdose." The last few words were but a whisper.

Her pain must be at a level he'd never experienced, yet
she still believed in and wanted a marriage, husband and
family. Misery filled him. That wasn't something he felt
he had the ability to give her, even if he wanted to. What
if he failed her? He cared too much to have her hurt like
that again.

It was time for a change in subject. Talk about something more pleasant. "Have you given any thought to dec-
orating the nursery? Especially since you know the sex
now."

"Not really…" Her voice trailed off as if she wasn't really listening.

"I wish you would. Will needs a place to come home to."

"Mmm..." Her head rested heavily against his shoulder.

Gabe just held her as she slept. A while later, he gently shook her. "Come on, sleepyhead. We need to go to bed."

"I didn't mean to go to sleep on you," she mumbled.

"Not a problem." He walked her inside.

Zoe headed toward her side of the house.

"Hey, where're you going?"

"To bed."

"Wrong way. You're with me." He extended his hand. For a second he worried she might not take it. To his relief, her palm met his. She curled her fingers around his as they walked to his bedroom. There he led her into the bath and turned on the shower, adjusting the water temperature.

"Are you getting a shower?" Zoe asked, her voice drowsy.

"We're getting a shower." Gabe begin to remove her clothes. She put up no resistance.

"You and me?"

Gabe grinned. She really was out of it. "Yes, honey, you and me." He cupped her face with his hands and kissed her before he turned her and opened the door to the shower stall. "In you go." Gabe gave her a gentle nudge at her waist before she stepped under the water.

He quickly removed his clothes and joined her. Zoe was so tired she was just standing beneath the water, letting it fall on her shoulders. They'd had an intense night the night before with little sleep. He picked up the soap and started washing her. She purred as his hands slid over her. He was deeply aroused but Zoe needed rest more than he needed release.

When she shivered, Gabe increased the temperature of the hot water and put her further under it. He quickly soaped up and rinsed. Cutting off the shower, he opened the door and jerked a towel off the rack. He dried Zoe and wrapped her in a towel. A minute later he'd dried, dropped his towel on the floor and guided Zoe to the bed. He jerked the spread back then removed the towel from Zoe. "Climb in, honey, before you chill."

She did as he said. Seconds later he joined her, pulling her to him and the covers snugly over them. In no time Zoe relaxed against him and was softly sleeping.

Contentment settled over him and he joined her.

The next evening when Gabe arrived home Zoe wasn't there.

The security he'd found in having her waiting for him was suddenly gone. How had she, in such a short time, managed to become such an important part of his life? He looked forward to coming home to her. The house was empty—not just the space, but the life force that made it a home was gone. Could he survive if she moved out?

An hour went by and still Zoe hadn't come home. Then another. He should have stayed at work. Guilt crept in. He had plenty of policies and procedures to read before he could start making serious changes to improve the program. He'd been leaving the hospital early far too often as it was to come home to see her. Now he was here and she wasn't.

As time went by, guilt turned to anger then to worry, which grew like a virus in a lab tube to the point where Gabe kept checking his phone, thinking he'd missed her call. More than once he'd stopped himself from phoning her because he had promised not to question her movements or try to control her. This anxiety and the waste of his time was drama he didn't need.

He loved having Zoe in his bed, but the emotionally draining side of their relationship would soon eat at him.

Might even affect his job. He couldn't have that. But letting Zoe go was unthinkable.

Relief flooded him at the sound of the garage door opening. She was home. He was waiting at the house door before she could get out of the car. Gabe said, more casually than he felt, "I've been worried about you."

"I went by to see Mom for a few minutes. Told her about William Gabriel, then did a little shopping for the nursery."

"You did?" Any residue of concern completely disappeared with the sound of happiness in her voice. At least the joy over the baby was overcoming her despair about her mother's health.

"Come and help me bring these packages in." Her head disappeared inside the car.

Gabe moved to stand beside her. She handed him a couple of huge plastic bags filled with fluffy items. "You did do some shopping."

"You said you'd like me to fix up the nursery. I got off a few minutes early today, so I thought I'd pick up some things."

"This is a little more than some." He chuckled as he headed toward the door of the house. His pleasure at seeing her and his relief over her being home safe made any discord he'd felt earlier disappear.

"Babies need a lot." Her tone held a defensive note.

"Hey, I was just kidding." He put the bags down in the hallway and wrapped his arms around her waist. "You can buy twice as much, for all I care."

Her hands were full of bags but her arms came around him anyway. "It was so much fun. I can hardly wait to show you what I got. I'm going to need your help."

"You've got it. Have you eaten yet?"

"No."

"Then why don't I fix us some breakfast for supper? You can sit at the table with your feet up for a while and tell me about your day and how your visit with your mother went." Who had he turned into? Nothing about those suggestions sounded like the person he thought he was. Zoe was changing him.

"That sounds great. Let me put these in the baby's room." She held up the bags in her hands. "I'm going to change into something more comfortable too."

"Sounds like a plan. I'll get started on dinner. Just leave these bags here and I'll get them later."

After eating, they spent the next two hours working in the nursery, and now Zoe sat on the floor, pulling open another package. She was dressed in baggy sweatpants and a shirt she had asked to borrow from him. Her skin was glowing, her eyes sparkled and she giggled as she showed him each new item. He couldn't think of a time she'd looked more amazing. But didn't he think that daily?

During the last hour he'd hung curtains under her direction and helped her place a bed skirt on the crib. He wasn't sure it was particularly useful but he didn't voice that out loud. All the time she had been chattering about her decision to get this or that and opening bags. Gabe didn't care one way or the other about any of it but he was enjoying listening to Zoe. Her excitement was infectious.

"This is the last thing." She opened the clear package and pulled out some material with a triumphant look.

"I have no idea what that is." It wasn't the first time he'd thought that about some of the objects she'd bought.

"It's a crib sheet."

"Oh." He nodded sagely. "Should have known that right

away. Hand it here and I'll put it on and that way you don't have to get up."

"Are you saying I can't?" There was a teasing note in her voice.

"No. I was just trying to be helpful. That's all."

"You weren't implying I was fat."

He grinned. "I know better than to do that."

"You'd better not."

After a struggle with the mattress and sheet that had Zoe giggling, Gabe finally had it in place. Done, he sat behind Zoe, spread his legs wide and wrapped her around her middle to bring her back until she rested against his chest. She placed her hands over his. He rested his chin on the top of her head.

He scanned the room, looking at the yellow and gray plaid curtains whose panels hung straight on either side of the windows, to the gray pillow with the yellow polka-dot cover, to the crib with a yellow sheet and the same plaid as the curtains on the bed skirt. He would have never thought to put those combinations together. He liked Zoe's taste. "So, are you pleased?"

"Hmm... I am. I still need to get a mobile and I want to do his name above the crib."

Gabe smiled. Her mind was still racing with ideas. "For someone who I had to talk into fixing up a nursery, you sure have run with it."

"It's fun, and you were right. Will needs a nice place to come home to."

But not live. There was that sick feeling in his gut again.

Zoe yawned.

"I think I need to get you to bed. You've had a long day." Gabe stood and then helped her up.

"I need to clean up this mess." She started to pick up a bag.

He took her hand. "Leave it until tomorrow." Gabe ushered her out of the room and turned off the light. He wanted her attention now.

Zoe was so tickled with the way the nursery had turned out. Gabe was a great help and even seemed to enjoy it. She hadn't even hesitated when he'd led her to his bedroom. In a few short nights she had started to think of it as hers. Sleeping without being in Gabe's arms would be impossible.

They were climbing into bed when he said, "I called my mother today. Told her what name we had decided on. I think she cried."

Zoe wasn't sure what to say to that. "She liked it, then?"

"She loved it. She said my father would be so proud." He gave Zoe a nudge to move further into the bed.

"What have you told your mother about me?"

"Nothing much really."

"She didn't ask any questions?" Zoe rolled to her side so she could see his face.

"I didn't say that."

Was he ashamed of her? Had he told his mother how easy Zoe had been to get into bed? She moved away from him. "Like what?"

"I told her your name. What you do for a living. That your mother is sick and you're wonderful with her. That sort of thing. Enough about her." He pulled Zoe toward him. "Let's think about us."

Zoe stopped his advance with a hand on his chest. Her look met his. She hated that she might ruin the happiness they had found together but she had to ask. "Gabe, what are we doing?"

"I don't know" was his soft reply. "Let's just see what happens."

For tonight she could accept that but for how long?

She was afraid that what happened would end up with her heart getting broken. Gabe drew her to him, giving her a deep kiss that had her thinking of nothing but what he made her body feel.

Their lovemaking had a desperate edge to it. As if what they had found they feared would soon disappear.

CHAPTER NINE

A WEEK LATER Zoe was on her way out of her office to make her weekly rounds to area hospitals. Her cell phone rang. Gabe's name showed on the screen.

She and Gabe had spent a blissful week together. They had taken walks, visited her mom, enjoyed the patio and spent precious moments in bed, many times just in each other's arms, talking. Yet there had been no more discussion of where their relationship was headed or what would happen after the baby was born. It was as if they were living in a bubble of happiness and they were the only ones who existed. They were pretending nothing would ever change, therefore no decisions needed to be made. Gabe's silence told her that he hadn't changed his mind about what his life would be. She couldn't accept less than what she wanted. They were living on borrowed time. Despite all that, her heart did a flip at the mere thought of him.

She touched the button.

"Hi, honey."

Would she ever get over the thrill of Gabe's voice calling her that? "Hey."

"I just received word there's a match for Mr. Luther."

"Really? That's wonderful." She couldn't believe it. So soon. The wait was usually much longer. The match must have been perfect.

"I've already made the call for him to come in. Hold

on a sec." Gabe spoke to someone else then said, "He should be on his way now. I expect to be in surgery late this evening."

"I'm on my way."

He hurriedly said, "I don't know if I'll have a chance to see you or not."

"I understand. I'll be busy with Mr. Luther anyway."

Gabe had been keeping exceptionally normal hours for the past week but she was sure that wouldn't always be the case. As often as possible, liver transplants were done during business hours, but there were always emergency situations. She worked in the medical field, understood that better than most. Tonight was an example.

Forty-five minutes later she arrived at the hospital and took the elevator up to the third floor, where the liver transplant unit was located. She went to the nurses' station and showed her credentials to the unit tech before requesting to look at Mr. Luther's chart. Zoe had just finished her review and was headed to his room when Gabe walked up.

He smiled. "Hey, I thought I'd miss you."

"Glad you didn't."

She glanced at the desk to find the unit clerk and a couple of nurses watching them.

"Come on. We'll go and see Mr. Luther." He put his hand on her back and directed her toward the other end of the hall.

At Mr. Luther's door she knocked. When there was no answer, she pushed the door open slightly. "Mr. Luther?"

The room was dark and the TV wasn't playing. Had the OR tech already come to get him? She moved further into the room with Gabe close behind. "Mr. Luther?"

A movement caught her attention. The man sat in a chair, looking out the window.

"Mr. Luther, it's Zoe. May I come in?"

"If you want."

It was as if all the blustery wind had gone out of the man. What was going on? "I needed to finalize some things before they come to take you to the OR. Dr. Marks is here too. May I turn the light on?"

"Please don't. I'm enjoying the sunset."

She knew that tone. It was the same one her father had used just before he'd left. The hopeless one. The one that said he had nothing to live for. Zoe wasn't going to let the same thing happen to Mr. Luther that had happened to her father.

She glanced back at Gabe then went to stand beside Mr. Luther. "Mind if I watch with you?"

"If you want to."

Gabe came to stand behind her. His hand came to rest on her waist. Would he have taken the time to do the same a few weeks ago?

The sky, already orange, slowly darkened to black. With the sun below the horizon, Gabe stepped back and she did too.

"I need to listen to you, Mr. Luther, before I have to go to the OR," Gabe said.

The man nodded and moved back to the bed. After he settled in, he focused on Gabe.

He pulled his stethoscope from around his neck. "You know, Mr. Luther, I'm good at what I do. I've done many liver transplants. I don't anticipate you having any problems."

"If you say so."

"I do. I want you to try not to worry." Gabe listened to Mr. Luther's heart.

"I thought if you didn't mind I'd stay right here with you," Zoe said as she stepped closer to the bed. "Maybe walk down to surgery with you. Would you mind?"

Mr. Luther, who had hardly had time for her when she'd visited, looked at her and smiled. "I'd like that."

"Zoe," Gabe said in a sharp voice and with a direct look. "It might run late."

She met his glare. "I know."

"You need to take care of yourself," Gabe insisted.

Mr. Luther nodded toward Gabe but looked at her and asked, "So what's the deal with you and the doctor here? That baby?"

Was their relationship that obvious? Apparently so. Under normal circumstances their conversation wouldn't have taken place in front of a patient. At least it had Mr. Luther thinking of something besides his impending surgery.

Zoe stared at Gabe. What should they say? How like Mr. Luther to ask such a direct personal question.

Gabe straightened. "Zoe is carrying my baby. We're having a boy."

She liked the pride she heard in his voice.

As if Gabe's statement had confirmed what he thought, Mr. Luther said, "Congratulations. Now, Doc, do you think you can put in that new liver?"

Zoe blinked at his change of attitude and subject.

"I can and I will. I'll see you in the OR." He looked at Zoe. "Can I speak to you in the hall?"

Zoe placed her hand on Mr. Luther's arm. "I'll be right back." She followed Gabe out the door.

"You shouldn't be spending long hours here," Gabe hissed before she could completely close the door. "I don't want to have to worry about you."

"I'll be fine. If I start feeling bad I'll get one of the security guards to walk me out if necessary. I'll just be in the waiting room." She glanced toward Mr. Luther's room. "He needs to know someone is here for him. I promise to only stay as long as I feel up to it."

"I guess there's no point in arguing with you." Gabe sounded resigned to the fact he couldn't fight her.

She smiled sweetly. "No, I don't think there is."

"Okay, but if you do leave, will you please text me and let me know you made it home?"

"I will. Thanks for caring."

Gabe's look captured hers. "I do, you know."

Joy flowed through her as hot as a beach in the summer. That was the closest Gabe had come to expressing his feelings. She smiled. "It's always nice to hear. I care about you too."

"Maybe we should talk about how much when I get home." He checked his watch. "I have to go. My team is waiting."

There was something about Gabe that hummed like electricity when he talked about doing surgery. His thoughts were already on the job ahead. He was in his element. Gabe knew how to save lives and did it well. She was proud of him. "I understand. I still have to do vitals on Mr. Luther."

He briefly touched her hand before walking away. Hope burned bright. Were her dreams coming true?

Gabe couldn't believe he had almost admitted to Zoe that he loved her in the middle of the hospital hallway. He had truly lost his mind where she was concerned. In his wildest dreams he would never have imagined opening his home to her would have also opened his heart. The last couple of weeks had been the most wonderful of his life. He'd never felt more content or cared for. Even going home had become more appealing than working late at the hospital. That had never entered his mind as a possibility or a desire before Zoe.

"Hello, ladies and gentlemen." He spoke to his transplant team less than an hour later. He was pleased with how they were slowly coming together to create an impressive group. "I appreciate all of you making it a late evening." With only their eyes visible over the masks they wore, they nodded. "This is our patient, Mr. Luther. He'll be getting a new liver today. Let's make sure he receives it in short order and with top care."

A couple of his staff gave him a questioning look. Gabe moved to stand beside the table. He said to the anesthesiologist, "Are we ready?"

"He's out and vitals stable," the woman answered.

"Scalpel," Gabe ordered.

His surgical nurse placed it in the palm of his hand. Seconds later Gabe went to work.

They were in the process of closing when the fellow, Dr. Webber, released a clamp.

"That needs to stay in place while we look for bleeders," Gabe said sharply.

"But this has been the process before," Dr. Webber replied.

"Not this time. I am trying a new procedure."

"Yes, sir." Dr. Webber replaced the clamp. "It's your patient and your call."

When Mr. Luther's incision had been closed, Gabe said, "Well done, everyone." He looked at the fellow. "Thank you. It's been nice working with you. I believe we have a world-class team here."

Despite the masks, he could see their smiles in their eyes. He left the OR and stepped into the next room to remove his surgical gown. A couple of the other staff followed.

"Nice job, Gabe," one of the team said.

"Thanks. I thought it went exceptionally smoothly." Gabe threw his gown in a basket.

"You were a little hard on the fellow in there, weren't you?" another said.

Gabe shrugged. "My OR, my call."

"Yeah, it was."

Gabe headed straight for the surgery waiting room to see if Zoe was still there. Hopefully she'd gone home, but if not, he could at least walk her to the car. He wasn't surprised to find she was still there.

Zoe stood and met him at the door. "Well, based on that smile on your face, everything went well."

"It did. There were no complications. Barring any infection, Mr. Luther should recover quickly and I anticipate him doing well with a much-improved quality of life."

She wrapped her arms around his waist and hugged him. "Thank you."

He pulled her close, not caring who might see them.

When Zoe eased away, he said, "Now it's time for you to go home. It's late. I have to stay a while longer, but I'm going to walk you to the car."

As they stood beside Zoe's car, Gabe pulled her into his arms and kissed her. Zoe gladly returned it. His kisses made her forget the noise of an ambulance approaching, cars on the nearby freeway whizzing along and the clang of a large truck going over a bump. There was nothing but Gabe.

There was a promise in his kiss. Something that hadn't been there before.

Gabe released her. "I'll be home as soon as I can. Now, in the car with you."

A little later, with a large yawn Zoe pulled into the carport and parked. It had been a long day. A few minutes later she climbed into what had become her and Gabe's bed. Tonight she missed his welcoming body next to hers.

Sometime later she was aware of the moment Gabe

slipped underneath the covers. The bed had gone from cool and lonely to warm and heavenly. He snuggled her in, just as he always did.

"What time is it?" she asked.

"Late."

"Mr. Luther?"

"In ICU and doing great. Now shush, go back to sleep." He kissed her forehead.

The next time Zoe woke, the morning sun was high and beaming into the bedroom windows. Gabe still snored softly next to her. She slowly slid out of his arms and from the bed. Picking up one of his shirts, she covered herself.

Knowing she would be out late, seeing about Mr. Luther, she had called the office and told them she wouldn't be in that day. She would go by the hospital and check on Mr. Luther later in the day. Zoe smiled. Since she lived with the transplant surgeon, she could get a personal update.

She'd just started the coffeepot so it would be ready when Gabe walked into the kitchen.

"Mornin'."

His voice was extra-low and gruff from sleep. Oh, so sexy.

She smiled. "Hey."

He took her in his arms. "Before you even ask, I just called the unit. Mr. Luther is doing great. They have already started weaning him off the respirator."

"I can't say thanks enough."

"Why don't you kiss me and we'll call it even." Gabe's head was already moving toward hers.

Her arms circled his neck and she eagerly went to him. She put all the love she felt into showing him how much.

As she pulled back, Gabe said, "You keep that up and I'll have to take you back to bed."

"I don't have a problem with that." She smiled at him.

He chuckled. "That's nice to hear but we should talk."

"Why don't we make breakfast first? Then we can talk while we eat." Zoe was already pulling a pan out of the cabinet.

"Sounds like a plan."

Half an hour later she and Gabe sat down at the table to what had turned into their favorite meal of eggs, bacon and toast.

Zoe had just picked up her fork when her phone rang. She looked at it. Shorecliffs. For them to be calling, something must be wrong with her mother. She answered.

"Ms. Avery, this is Ms. Marshall."

"Yes?"

"I'm sorry to have to tell you this but your mother is missing."

"What!" Panic shot through Zoe, mixed with disbelief and shock. She looked at Gabe, who had stopped eating and wore a concerned look.

"One of the new employees left a door propped open and she walked out. We have it on video. We're searching for her now. I have called the police. I wanted to let you know in case she comes to you."

No one would be at the apartment. Her mother wouldn't remember that Zoe now lived with Gabe.

Zoe stood. "I'll help look. Please keep me informed."

"We will. Again, I'm sorry about this."

Zoe ended the call. To Gabe she said, "Mom's missing. I have to go."

Before he could respond his phone buzzed. Zoe rushed to her bedroom, already stripping off Gabe's shirt as she went. Where could her mother be? What if she was hurt? Guilt assaulted Zoe. Her mother should be living with her. Instead, Zoe was busy playing "happy home" with Gabe.

He came to the door. "Tell me what happened."

As she pulled on clothes, she told him what the woman had said. "I'm going to the old apartment to see if she's there, even though I can't imagine how she would get there."

Gabe came closer. "That call was from the hospital. There's an emergency and I'm needed. I'm sorry but I can't go with you. I have to see about this."

Zoe glared at him. "What? My mother is missing. You aren't going to help me look for her?"

He gave her an imploring look. "I've got to go. It's my responsibility."

"Couldn't someone else fill in for you just for a little while?"

"I'm the head of the department. It's my job."

"Go. Do what you need to do. If you're needed, you're needed." She pulled on her pants. But she needed him too. Still, his job was important. It hurt that he couldn't be there for her. When had she last been this scared? When her father had left.

"You take care of yourself. Don't do anything crazy. She has to be near the home."

"You don't know that. She could be anywhere!" Zoe lashed back. She jerked her shoes on.

"Call me the second you find her."

Zoe pushed past him and hurried down the hall toward the garage. "Okay. I've got to go and find my mother."

Gabe shook his head. As nice as the day had started, with Zoe sharing his bed and the plans he'd had for them coming to an understanding about the future, it had all turn upside down and ugly with two quick calls. He had left the house with the thought he would clear up the problem at the hospital and join Zoe in the search, but it didn't work out that way.

When he arrived at the hospital, he soon learned the

patient would need surgery and he was the most qualified to perform it. Any hope he held of being at Zoe's side
slipped away.

Going into the OR, he told the unit tech, "Please let me
know if I get any messages."

She gave him a curious look but nodded. "Yes, Doctor."

Most of the time he left a "Do Not Disturb" request.
This time he was worried about not only Zoe but her
mother.

It was a couple of hours later while Gabe was busy su-
turing the vein that had been bleeding that the OR phone
rang. A nurse answered and relayed a message. "Dr.
Marks, the mother has been found. She is well."

Gabe didn't let himself falter as he continued to work,
but relief washed over him, along with sadness. He wasn't
there to support Zoe. She must be so relieved. Her desperation and fear had been written all over her face but
he had still left her in her time of need. It gnawed at him.
She'd needed him then and now, and he wasn't there for
her. Would be, if he truly cared. Zoe should be the number one thing in his life, always come first.

The very thing he'd feared the most and had tried to
avoid had happened. He'd proved he was right about himself. He had chosen his career over her. For him, his profession and a family didn't mix. He didn't know how to
make them mesh. Others could do it, he'd seen it, but he
just wasn't capable of doing it. He'd not even grown up
watching a marriage. And to think he had started to believe he could have one. Zoe had made him care enough
to want to try. But now...

On his way home he made a decision. He had to let her
go. For her sake, she needed to find a man who could give
her what she needed. Today had just been an example of
how he wasn't that person. Zoe deserved better than him.
He would be there for Will, but Zoe wanted more from

their relationship than he could give. It might kill him but he would have to let her go.

It was turning dark before he pulled into the drive. The lights shone brightly in the house. Zoe was waiting for him. He had no doubt of that. There would be a hot meal there as well. His chest ached for what had been and what he was about to do. Her day must have been emotionally exhausting yet she'd thought about him. Zoe had such a capacity to love. Her mother, he himself and Mr. Luther were all evidence of that, and soon Will would be.

Gabe pulled into the garage, cut off the engine but didn't get out immediately. He needed to gather his thoughts, think through what he was going to do. He couldn't continue to live in the house with Zoe. Having her so close and not being able to touch her would slowly drive him mad. He would have to move out. Go stay in a hotel. No way would he ask her to go. The baby was only weeks away. She wouldn't like the idea but he would make her accept it.

He slammed his hand down on the steering wheel. This was just the drama he wanted no part of. The kind that would steer him away from his goals. Made him think of other things besides his career.

The door to the house opened. Zoe was silhouetted there. Oh, heaven help him, he was going to miss her. He climbed out of the car.

"Hey, are you all right?" she called.

"Fine. Just on my way in." Gabe stepped closer to her. "Tell me about what happened with your mom."

She smiled and headed toward the kitchen as he closed the garage door. "Thank goodness it sounded worse than it was. She did leave the home but didn't get far. The door she went out of was the one to the garden area. They found her in the potting shed, filling pots with soil. You were right. She was close by. I'm sorry I acted so irrationally. I shouldn't have demanded you stay with me."

"They didn't look there before calling you or the police?" Anger filled Gabe at the distress they had caused Zoe.

"Someone had, but apparently my mother had stepped around to the back of the shed to look for something to dig with and they missed her. On the second pass, there she was."

"I'm sorry they scared you."

They continued into the kitchen.

"I have to admit all kinds of things were running through my head at what could go wrong." She stopped near the sink and turned to face him. "I fixed supper. Thought we could eat out on the patio tonight. You hungry?"

He was. For her more than anything. "Yeah."

"Then you go wash up while I get it on the table."

Gabe went to his room. Zoe had no idea what was coming. Her mother's successful return hadn't changed his mind. If something like that happened again, where would he be? Beside Zoe or off seeing to a stranger? No, he couldn't do that to her again.

When he returned to the kitchen, Zoe wasn't there. She waved to him from outside where she sat at the patio table, waiting for him.

"I just filled our plates. Simpler that way. I hope you don't mind."

"No." There was little he minded about Zoe. As far as he was concerned, she was near perfect.

The weight of what he was about to say made each of his steps feel as if he were wearing lead shoes. Nothing in his life had been more difficult. He would wait until they had eaten before he explained how it must be. At least they could share this last meal.

As he settled in his chair, Zoe asked, "So how's your patient doing?"

How like Zoe after the day she'd had to show concern for someone else. "She's stable and should recover without any issues."

"I'm sure that's due to your superior skills." She nibbled at a roll.

It didn't make what he had to do any easier, hearing her vote of confidence. "I have a good team." He took a bite of the chicken she had prepared. "This is good. Thanks for going to the trouble after the day you've had."

"Not a problem. After things were settled with Mother and I calmed down, it turned into a perfectly nice day."

Which he was getting ready to ruin. Suddenly his food had no taste. "What kind of arrangements did Shorecliffs make for what happened this morning not to occur again?"

Zoe took a sip of the hot tea she was having. "They were going to fire the guy that propped the door open but I told them that wasn't necessary. It had scared him enough that he won't do it again."

"You're a better person than I am." He had no doubt she was.

"I don't know about that."

When they finished their meal, Zoe stood and picked up their plates. "I made a pie as well. Want some?"

He'd put off what needed doing long enough. "Maybe later. Leave those. I'd like to talk to you for a minute."

Zoe put the plates down, sank into her chair and clasped her hands over her middle. He held her attention. "I know we promised to talk but—"

"Zoe, please..."

Confusion filled her eyes and she pursed her lips. "What's going on, Gabe?"

"This—" he waved a hand between them "—isn't working for me."

"What're you talking about?" Her voice was flat as fear replaced confusion in her eyes.

"I've been leading you to believe that our relationship is moving toward something more permanent. It can't."

"You said you care about me." She watched him closely, as if searching for the truth.

"I do."

"So what does that mean?" Zoe's eyes narrowed.

He shrugged both shoulders. "That I care about what happens to you. To the baby."

"I don't get it."

Gabe wasn't surprised. He wasn't making any sense. "I'm not who you need."

"Isn't that my choice?"

He wasn't sure how to answer that. "Yes," Gabe said with hesitation. "But I'm not going to let you."

Zoe straightened her shoulders, glared at him. The stubborn look he knew so well came over her face. She was no longer on the defensive; she was taking the offensive position. "For a man of your intelligence you aren't making any sense. Just what's the problem? Tell me."

"I can't be there for you like I should be. I've been pretending for the last couple of weeks. I had thought we could make a real go of it, but this morning just proved I'd been right all along."

"And just how's that?" Her tone had turned patronizing.

"My career, my choices would always go to my patients. Your mother was missing and I get a call from the hospital and choose them over being with you. A real relationship is about caring for the other person. I let you down."

"So you think I'm weak?"

His eyes narrowed. What was her point? "I didn't say that."

"I believe that's what you meant. You think I can't handle something like what happened today with Mother on my own. I've been doing that for years. Just because you came into my life, it doesn't mean I still can't. You had a patient who needed you today. I understand that." She pointed to her chest. "Remember, I work in the medical field too. I get it better than most women do."

"But I should have been there to support you."

"Next time you will be. Today you were needed else-where. You had a good reason."

"But you're the one who told me you wanted a husband and a family. Isn't that what someone does when they're a husband, be there for the other person?"

"Sure they do. When they can. As for what I want, mostly it's for someone to love me."

"I'm not that guy." The devastation that filled her eyes almost had him on his knees, begging her to forgive him. But he'd never be the man for her. "You expect a marriage to be perfect. I don't even know how to do marriage. Today proves it. I'd make a horrible husband."

"Sure seems like the last couple of weeks you've been doing a fine job of playing the part. Everything about our day-to-day lives looked like a marriage. The neighbors even thought so. Were you just playacting?"

Gabe didn't want to answer that question. He hadn't been, but if he told her that then he'd offer her hope. "Zoe, it's just not going to work."

"You didn't answer the question, Gabe."

He pushed back from the table. "No, I wasn't pretend-ing." Why couldn't she just accept what he was telling her and let them move on? Zoe reached out but he pulled back. If he allowed her to touch him, she would melt his resolve.

"Gabe, forget all the shouldn'ts and let loose. We can make this work together. Let yourself feel. Trust me enough to love you. I do. I have for a long time."

He could hardly breathe. Was a truck running over his

chest? One slight woman had a hold on his heart and was squeezing. "I've let things get out of hand. I knew this would happen. I shouldn't be putting you through this. My patients will always come first. You don't deserve that."

"Don't I get to decide that too? I understand you're a doctor."

"You shouldn't have to. I want better for you."

"Do you really? Or is that the excuse you're using?" She paused then looked at him as if she'd realized something. "Oh, I get it. I've just been one in the long list of people you feel you need to help. Your patients, strangers in airports, your child. You took me in because you're a good guy. That's it. It has had nothing to do with loving me. It must be hard to carry all those needs of the world on your shoulders and still not let yourself feel. Such a burden." Her tone dripped sarcasm. "How noble, and unnecessary. The problem is you do care. You know, Gabe, I would've never have thought you, of all people, would be running scared."

Gabe jerked to his feet. He'd taken all he could. Right now he didn't like her and liked himself even less. It must be this way. He loved her too much to fail her like her father had, and he would if they continued down the road they were traveling. The sudden need to get away clawed at him.

He'd had enough. Of Zoe. Of what could have been.

"We're done here. I'm going to move to a hotel. I want you to stay here as planned until after the baby is born. Hell, keep the place, for all I care." He stalked off.

Zoe called to his back as tears spilled, "I don't need noble. I need your love."

She had told Gabe the truth when she'd said she understood about that morning. It wasn't as if he had chosen to watch a ball game over going with her. His surgical skills had been required. In her heart she'd known he would be there beside her if he could have been. Frustration rolled through her. Why couldn't he see that?

What was she going to do now? Chase after him and beg him to reconsider? She couldn't do that but she was living in his home. That couldn't continue. She would have to find a place sooner than she'd planned. What about her mother? She wouldn't survive a second move. Zoe would have to figure something out. To put Gabe out of his house would be wrong. Staying here without him would be just as impossible. The memories would be more than she could stand.

She picked up the dishes and carried them to the sink. The sound of the door to the carport opening and closing screamed that Gabe had left. Zoe's hands covered her face and she let the tears of misery flow.

CHAPTER TEN

IT HAD BEEN two weeks since Gabe had driven out of the driveway, his intention to only return for clothes later. His contact with Zoe would only have to do with the baby after it was born. He couldn't continue seeing her and keep his promise to stay away. He wasn't even sure it wouldn't be a good idea for him to sell the house when she moved out. Facing the memories might be more than he could manage. It would never be home again unless Zoe was there.

Just seeing her would make his resolve disappear like mist on a sunny day.

Gabe couldn't imagine being more miserable than he had been over the last couple of weeks. He'd missed everything about what his life had once been and it all hinged on Zoe. The way she looked when he called her honey. Or her laughter as he told her something that had happened at work, the joy in her eyes when she'd heard Mr. Luther was doing well. The unconscious way she'd put a protective hand over their baby when they'd talked about it.

Shoving the take-out paper bag away, he groaned. He missed her delicious meals and their simple conversations. She'd been what had been absent in his life, and now that he'd had her, he wanted her back. His personal life was in a shambles.

It was starting to affect his work. The lack of sleep because he was living in a hotel and didn't have Zoe was starting to take its toll. A couple of his coworkers had given him questioning looks when he said something too sharply. He tried to remember to think before he spoke but it didn't always work.

It was Tuesday and his clinic day. He wasn't looking forward to seeing the next patient. He lightly knocked on the door. A gruff voice called for him to come in. As he entered the small room, Gabe said, "Hello, Mr. Luther. How're you doing?"

"Better. The scar doesn't hurt as much as it used to."

Gabe nodded. "Good. That sounds like you're making progress."

The man had only stayed a few days in ICU and had been out of the hospital in less than a week. Gabe had seen Zoe's name beside notes on Mr. Luther's chart a few times but Gabe hadn't run into her. He couldn't keep dodging her but he needed a little more time to adjust to what his life was now.

"I feel better than I have in years. My neighbors are taking good care of me."

"I'm glad to hear that. I'm going to give you a good listen then look at the incision site." A few minutes later Gabe said, "Every day you should be improving and you're doing that. I'll see you back here in a couple of weeks. Is there anything you have questions about?"

"Yeah. I'd like to know what you did to Zoe. She looks sad all the time."

Gabe's chest ached. Of course, Mr. Luther would notice. "How is she?"

"Why don't you ask her yourself?"

"It's complicated." Gabe stepped toward the door.

"That's what she said. One thing I've learned through all this is that life can slip away before you know it. Think about it, Doc."

Gabe did regularly over the next few days. Still, he

couldn't see how things could be any different. For Zoe to find that man who could give her what she wanted, she couldn't have Gabe hanging around. Even the idea of Zoe being with another man made him feel physically sick. Surely with time it would get easier, but so far that didn't seem to be the case.

While in his office that evening, his phone rang. He looked at the ID. "Hi, Mom."

"Hey, Gabe. I've not heard from you in a few weeks."

"I'm sorry, Mom. I've been busy." He sounded so much like his mother used to when he was a child, never having enough time when he wanted to talk.

"So how's Zoe and the baby doing?"

"Fine."

There was a pause. "What's going on, Gabe?"

"Nothing I can't handle." He wished he felt as confident as he sounded.

"I'm here if you need me."

She might have worked a lot when he had been a kid, but he'd always known she was there to support him. With or without a father, his mother had been there when she could be. "Mom, why did you never remarry?"

Again there was a pause. This one was longer than the last. "I guess I never found the right man. Your father was a hard act to follow. Then I just got too busy. I worry that you're doing the same. I learned too late that you can't make more time. Don't let it slip by. Especially with the little guy coming."

"I heard you say once that you were worried I had no father figure to model myself on."

"I did?" Amazement was evident in her voice. "Single mothers worry about all kinds of things. Big and small. Gabe, you're one of the most intelligent, caring, giving men I know. I have no doubt that my grandson will have the best father ever."

A sense of relief came over Gabe. His mother believed in him. Hadn't Zoe said close to the same thing? So why couldn't he believe in himself?

"By the way, I'm planning to come for the birth," his mother added. "Help out. Is that okay?"

"I'll have to check with Zoe." He wasn't prepared to go into all the details about his and Zoe's relationship with his mother at that moment. He would have to sometime soon but he wasn't up to explaining it right now. Even if his mother came, she'd have to stay in a hotel and see the baby through a window.

How was he going to explain what had happened between him and Zoe? His mother had been so excited when he'd told her he'd found someone special. When he told her he and Zoe were no longer together, his mother would be so disappointed. "It's great to talk to you, Mom. I'll see you soon."

Zoe wasn't sure her heart would ever completely recover. The pain she'd feared would come with the loss of Gabe was nowhere near as strong as that she was carrying now. Her days had become a foggy existence. Every night was a struggle without Gabe next to her and every morning an act of survival to meet the day. She had become reliant on him so quickly and now he wasn't there.

Going home daily to Gabe's house compounded the pain but she had no choice. She couldn't move her mother, and the only way Zoe could afford a new place was to move her mother. So she was stuck living at Gabe's. It seemed wrong that she was and he wasn't. Her life had become so twisted. At least she'd just have to endure for a few more months. The only bright spot in the mess her life had become was that Will would arrive soon. That she could get excited about.

Had Gabe changed his mind about his involvement with

Will? Had he broken it off not only with her but their child as well? He'd been so adamant about being involved, but with the change in their relationship, had he decided staying away was better? That decision was his. Gabe would have to approach her about it, not the other way around.

Because of Will, she and Gabe would always be connected. She would have to figure out some way to control her emotions when they had to meet. Even though she was certain a little bit of her would die each time they did, knowing the happiness she'd once shared with Gabe was gone.

At her obstetrician visit, the doctor was concerned about her weight loss. She promised to take better care of herself. Only with great effort did she make herself eat and do what was necessary for the baby's health.

She'd not heard or seen Gabe since he'd left. The day he'd come to pick up his clothes, she'd noticed his car in the drive and had driven around the neighborhood until it had gone. Now she'd do almost anything for a glimpse of him. Even when she visited Mr. Luther she'd not seen Gabe.

It didn't take Mr. Luther long to zoom in on her unhappiness. As she would have guessed, he commented on it.

"What's wrong with you?" he asked as she wrapped the blood-pressure cuff around his arm.

"Nothing."

"Yeah, there is. You've got that pitiful look. Usually you come in here with a smile on your face. I bet your face would break if you smiled right now."

"I think we should concentrate on how you're doing." She pumped the bulb attached to the cuff.

For once Zoe wished Mr. Luther would go back to being the sad, self-centered man she'd known before the transplant. At least he wouldn't be focused on her.

"You know, the doc doesn't look much happier when he comes in."

He didn't? Why did the idea make Zoe's heart beat a little fast? Maybe Gabe was as miserable as she was. Zoe continued to do vitals. "I'm sorry to hear that."

"You two have a fight or something?"

"Mr. Luther, I appreciate your concern, but Dr. Marks and I are fine."

He grunted. "Don't look fine to me. That baby deserves happy parents."

That statement Zoe couldn't argue with.

On the way home that afternoon, she stopped by to visit her mother. Now that Gabe wasn't at the house, Zoe had made a habit of going each afternoon. Going home to Gabe's house wasn't comforting for her. It was just a place to lay her head, no longer the place of dreams it had once been.

With the exception of the one escape episode, her mother seemed to have stabilized and was thriving since moving to Shorecliffs. She seemed more aware, and despite most of what she talked about being in the past, it at least made sense. With her confusion remaining at bay for the time being, Zoe's guilt had eased. Her mother was as happy as she could be.

Today her mom was well dressed and sitting in a cushioned chair in the lobby. There were a number of other residents there as well. Zoe took an empty chair beside her. "Hey, Mom, how're you today?"

Her mother smiled.

The tightness in Zoe's shoulders eased. Her mother was having a good day. There was a sparkle in her eyes, not the dull look of reality slipping away. "I'm fine. How're you?"

Zoe ran her hand over her extended middle. "Me too."

"Baby?" her mother asked.

"Yes, I'm having a baby." Zoe had to remind her almost every visit. Anything that had happened recently her mother couldn't remember, but she could recall almost anything in detail from her childhood. "He's growing."

"Your daddy and I had a big fight about you."

Was she making that up? Zoe had never heard this story. To her knowledge, they had never fought.

"He was mad when I told him I was going to have a baby. He didn't want a family." Her mother's face took on a faraway look.

"Mom, I've never heard you say anything like that before."

"That's not something you tell a child. A baby should be wanted. Loved."

A deep sadness filled her. "He didn't want me?"

"After you came he loved you dearly, but he never adjusted to family life. He was always looking for a way out."

Was she expecting Gabe to embrace an ideal he wanted nothing to do with? Was she asking the impossible from him? Was that why he had left? They had been happy together for two weeks without more commitment. Could she settle for that if it meant having Gabe in her life? Her child having a full-time father?

Was there some way she could convince Gabe she would take him any way she could get him? Make him feel like what he could give was plenty.

Gabe searched the patient's open abdomen. Something was wrong. He could feel it.

"Suction." He looked again. Nothing. The surgery was going by the textbook. So why the nagging feeling?

The phone on the OR wall rang. One of the nurses answered. "Dr. Marks." The nurse held out the receiver. "Do you know a Zoe Avery?"

"Yes. Why?" Was the baby coming? It was too early. It was at least another six weeks away.

"This is the ER calling."

Gabe's heart went into his throat.

The nurse continued, sounding perplexed. "They said they found your card in her purse. She'd had a bad car accident."

Zoe hurt! The baby?

Gabe looked at Dr. Webber standing on the other side of the surgery table. He was more than qualified to handle the rest of the operation. Gabe had to get out of there. See about Zoe. He spoke to the fellow. "You've got this. I gotta go." Gabe didn't wait for a response before he hurried out the doors, leaving them swinging. Zoe needed him and he would be there for her and Will this time.

He flipped his surgical headlamp up on his head and didn't bother to remove his gown as he raced toward the staff stairs that would get him the two flights down faster than the elevator. Less than a minute later he burst through the ER doors, one of them hitting the wall.

"Whoa," one of the techs said as he put his hand out to stop Gabe. "Can I help you, Doctor?"

Gabe pushed the man's arm away. "Where's Zoe Avery?"

"Let me check the board." The tech turned to the large whiteboard on the wall. "Trauma Six."

Gabe looked around wildly. "Where's that?"

"This way. You must be new here. Were you called in to consult?"

"No. She's my...uh..." What did he call Zoe? His friend, girlfriend, lover, the mother of his baby? Thankfully he didn't have to explain more before they reached the room. Gabe rushed inside.

His heart sank and his belly roiled. The stretcher was surrounded by people working on Zoe. Two different monitors beeped, one giving Zoe's heart rate and the other the baby's. Oxygen hissed as the doctor gave orders.

With his gut churning with fear at what he might see, Gabe stepped closer. "Zoe." Her name was barely a whisper over his lips.

The doctors and nurses were so busy they didn't even respond to him. Gabe looked over one of their shoulders. Zoe's eyes were closed and she wore an oxygen mask. Around it and beneath he could see her pale, bruised skin. Her right arm lay to her side with an air cast on it. The real focus was on Zoe's leg. There was a large gash on her thigh.

"We need to get her to surgery, stat. She's lost a lot of blood. Do we have a next of kin?"

"I'm it," Gabe said. "She's my girlfriend."

The ER doctor turned and looked up and down at Gabe. "Aren't you Dr. Marks?"

"I am."

"Okay. Let's get her up to the OR," the doctor ordered. To Gabe he said, "You take care of the paperwork and the surgeon will be out to speak to you in the waiting room."

"I'll see him in Recovery," Gabe shot back. He watched helplessly as Zoe was pushed away. The first chance he had to tell her how he felt about her he was going to. If she would have him, he'd promise to do whatever he could to make her happy.

Zoe worked at opening her eyes. Why were they so heavy? Someone held her hand. She shifted. That hurt.

"Don't move, honey."

That voice. She knew that voice. *Gabe.*

Dreaming, that was what she was doing. Her eyes fluttered closed.

Zoe woke again and blinked as the lights were so bright. Where was she?

"Honey, stay still."

There was Gabe again. He sounded worried. Why? "Gabe?"

"Right here." His hand squeezed hers as his face came into view.

"You're here." *He was here.*

"I am, and I'm never leaving you again." He kissed her forehead.

All the pain of the last few weeks washed away. Gabe was next to her. Touching her. Calling her honey. What had happened? Why did he look so scared?

A nurse moved around her bed, checking the IV lines and doing vitals. "Ms. Avery, we're getting ready to move you to your room."

When the nurse left, Zoe searched Gabe's face. "What happened?"

"You were in a car accident."

The haze started to clear. She'd been driving home and had been hit from behind. The next thing she'd known, she was being slammed into the car in front of her. Tears filled her eyes. Zoe reached for her middle with her un-injured hand. "Will?"

"Shh, honey. Our baby is just fine." Gabe's hand came to rest over hers.

Zoe drifted off again.

When she woke next, it was dark outside and she was in a hospital room. She looked around. Her eyes focused on Gabe, who was sitting in a chair facing her. His hand held hers as if it was a lifeline. "Gabe."

He straightened quickly. "Right here. Is something wrong? How are you feeling?"

"I ache all over."

Gabe stood, but didn't let go of her hand. "I'm not surprised. You're lucky it wasn't worse. I saw pictures of the accident." His voice hitched with emotion. "I could have lost you both."

She squeezed his fingers. "We're right here. My leg hurts."

Gabe's doctor persona returned. "You have a broken arm and had a deep laceration on your thigh. Both were taken care of in surgery."

Zoe looked at her arm, which was in a cast. Tears threatened to spill over. "I won't be able to take care of Will when he comes."

"With any luck, it'll be off before then. Either way, I'll be there to help."

"You will?" She watched him closely. Did he really mean it? But he'd never lied to her, only to himself.

"I can't wait any longer to say this. I'm sorry for how I treated you. You were right. I was just afraid. Still am. I know nothing more about being a husband or a father than I did before, but what I do know is that I can't live without you. I promise to put you and our family above anything else in my life. If you'll just have me. I love you, Zoe."

Gabe's plea squeezed her heart. "Of course I will have you. I love you."

His lips found hers. The kiss was tender but held a promise of many to come.

They were interrupted by a nurse entering the room. While she was seeing about Zoe, Gabe stepped out into the hallway. As soon as the nurse was finished, Gabe re-entered the room.

"Why're you wearing a surgical gown?" Zoe asked.

Gabe gave her a sheepish grin. "When they called me about you, I was in surgery. I left in the middle of the procedure and didn't stop to change."

He had? "You shouldn't have done that."

"Yes, I should. I'll always be there whenever you need me somehow or some way. I won't leave you again."

"Gabe, your work is important. It saves lives. I understand that." Zoe could only imagine the drama he'd caused.

"I left the patient in good hands. He's doing fine. I just checked in."

"I love you," Zoe mumbled.

"I love you more," she heard as she slipped off into sleep once more.

She had no idea how much time had passed when she woke again, but Gabe was still there beside her. He was leaning back in the chair with his eyes closed. His long legs were stretched out in front of him and his ankles crossed. Zoe couldn't take her eyes off him. He was such an amazing man with such a large capacity to love. And he'd chosen her. She was blessed.

"You're staring at me." Gabe opened his eyes and smiled at her. "How're you feeling?"

"Pain meds are a good thing."

"Yes, they can be." He stood.

Zoe didn't miss his professional habit of checking all the monitors and lines before his attention returned to her. "Gabe, you know you don't have to stay here with me. You need to go home and get some rest."

"My home is right here. You are it."

Her heart melted. If he hadn't already owned her heart, he would have after that statement.

"What made you change your mind about us?" She had to know. Believe that it wasn't just because of the accident.

"Honey, I've been miserable without you. Nothing has been right. It was even starting to be noticed at work. No hospital needs a lovesick surgeon heading a transplant program. And I spoke to my mother. When I was a kid I overheard her say something about me not having a role model for fatherhood. She didn't even remember saying it. That seed grew in my mind to the point I believed it."

"You have so many qualities that'll make you a great father."

"I think with you at my side I can be." He kissed her.

"Zoe, I know this isn't the best time to ask this but I need to know—will you marry me?"

Gabe was everything she'd ever wanted in a husband but she didn't need marriage to prove they loved each other. "You don't want to get married. I understand that. Accept it."

"Yes, I do. I want people to know you belong to me. I want my son and any more children we have to carry my name. I love you."

"My mother had a lucid moment and we had a conversation about Daddy. It seems he never wanted a family, felt strangled by one. I don't want you to ever feel that way. If not being married is what works for you, then I'll be satisfied just to be in your life."

Gabe leaned over until his face was near hers. "I love you and *want* to marry you. Now, will you please answer my question? I'll beg if I have to."

With effort and some discomfort, Zoe circled his neck with her good arm. "Yes, I will marry you. I love you." Her lips found his.

EPILOGUE

GABE LEFT HIS mother in his kitchen, fussing with dinner, and went to find Zoe. He stopped in the nursery doorway and looked at the picture Zoe and their baby made as they slowly rocked in the sunshine. A glow that could only be love radiated from Zoe as she looked down at the perfect baby boy in her arms. His family.

She must have heard him because she looked up with an angelic smile and met his gaze. The love he'd just seen for Will was now transferred to Gabe. It didn't waver. What he'd done to earn it, he had no idea. The thing he did know was he would spend the rest of his life honoring it.

"Hey, honey." Zoe's smile grew, just as it always did at his endearment.

"Come in and join us. Your son would like to say hi."

Gabe walked to them and gently kissed Zoe on the forehead. "You did well, Mrs. Marks."

"Thank you, Dr. Marks. I think we both did well." Gabe carefully took Will from her, cradling him against his chest. Zoe's cast had only been removed a few days earlier.

Gabe looked at the peachy chubby face and he worried his heart might burst from the amount of love filling it. "Hello, William Gabriel Marks."

Zoe rose to stand beside him.

He looked at her, at the tears filling her eyes. His lips found hers. "I love you."

"And I love you."

"Just think, in my stupidity I almost missed out on this."

She leaned her head against his shoulder. "But you didn't and that's what matters."

* * * * *

LET'S TALK

Romance

For exclusive extracts, competitions
and special offers, find us online:

f facebook.com/millsandboon

⊙ @millsandboonuk

🐦 @millsandboon

Or get in touch on 0844 844 1351*

For all the latest titles coming soon,
visit millsandboon.co.uk/nextmonth